# THE

# DINKA

# FOLKTALES

*Jacob Manyuon Dhieu Chol*

*A Note from the Publisher*

The publisher wishes to acknowledge and thank Dr Douglas H. Johnson for his invaluable help and support for Africa World Books and its mission of preserving and promoting African cultural and literary traditions and history. Dr Johnson and fellow historians have been instrumental in ensuring that African people remain connected to their past and their identity. Africa World Books is proud to carry on this mission.

© 2017 Jacob Manyuon Dhieu Chol

ISBN  978-0-6452105-9-0
First Edition Published January 2017
Second Edition July 2017

Cover design, typesetting and layout : Africa World Books

I dedicate this book to my kids and the youth;
our hope for the future.

# Table of Contents

# Foreword

—————◦⟨◦⟩◦—————

Culture is a set of social codes governing values, norms and behaviors held consciously or unconsciously by groups of people. The Dinka cultural heritage and ways of life have been, and will always inevitably continue to be, with our children and the generations to come. Storytelling about folktales, fables, animal lore, folklores, folk songs, myths, fairy tales and legends are common amongst the Dinka communities as well as other African tribes. The stories are generally narrated by elders to the children as they sit around a fireplace in the evenings. More so some individuals were so crafty in storytelling that they were respected as good story-tellers full of humor and wisdom.

It isn't possible to trace the authorship of any of the stories recorded in this book. When a Dinka storyteller is questioned about authorship, they say that they orally acquired stories from their ancestors, and the same story, or parts of it may be found in other sections of the Nilotic communities.

In this book, *The Dinka Folktales: A collection of Dinka's Short Stories and Mythologies,* the Dinka mythologies: myths, legends and folktales have been collated purposefully to be learned as history by future generations. These stories are extremely diverse and heterogeneous; they convey customs and our ways of life as their themes and motives give us an overview of African traditional cultural heritage and diversity, especially of the Dinka community.

These oral traditions were passed down from generation to generation. The myths explain the actions of gods, heroes and natural occurrences, while legends tell about the past stories that may or may not be based on facts and the folktales entertain us about heroes, adventures, or mischief-makers. Folktales and myths offer fictional explanations for natural occurrences.

I believe both the scholars and students of the Dinka tribe and other African communities will find this book useful . Some of these tales will make you think, laugh, wonder, but almost all of them have hidden wisdom for you to discover! Although a lot remains to be done, the author has demonstrated to us that there are more hidden oral traditions to be discovered.

In this book, animals, birds and human beings are the main characters; clever foxes and hares, bewitching owls, diplomatic rabbits, greedy hyena, brave lions or tigers and forgetful dogs.

As Samuel Huntington puts it, "The most important distinctions amongst people are not ideological, political, or economic viewpoints, it is the cultural norms. Peoples from various nations are attempting to answer the most basic question human beings face: Who are we? And they are answering the question in traditional ways that suit their cultural and social backgrounds, reference to the things that mean most for them. People define themselves in terms of ancestry, religion, language, history, values, customs and institutions."

# Acknowledgements

Invariably, such an oral tradition reconstruction process as in this book calls for a collective responsibility from several knowledgeable individuals. First and foremost, I recognize my late grandpa, Zachariah Chol Majok and my late father, Abraham Dhieu Chol Majok for retelling us the stories. I offer my sincerest appreciation and gratitude to Makwei Mabioor Deng, Awuol Arok Kiir, William Kon Chol Tuet and Dau Atem Dau for devoting a lot of their time proof-reading, editing and formatting this book. I'm grateful to you all and have no words to describe the happiness and the enormous joy you have left in my heart.

Secondly, I thank my benevolent mother-in-law, Canon Mary Achol Deng Ajang Awai, my great mum, Reverend Daruka Abuk Thon Mayen, my caring brothers: Mabior Dhieu, Kuany Dhieu, Thon Dhieu, Majok Dhieu, my beloved wife, Elizabeth Nyanlang Deng Lual and my esteemed sisters, Amam Dhieu and Amam Mabior for acting as my close wise counsels who get me back on track whenever I waver while compiling the tales after *Tiördekuëi* had passed on. I love you my people more than you would ever know, and I still remember your kind words and humility whenever you retell the folktales.

In a nutshell, to friends, colleagues and relatives whose names have not been mentioned here, I wholeheartedly acknowledge you for your usual support and encouragement. Thank you, all my people for your constant collaboration and unwavering support to make this

xii Jacob Manyuon Dhieu Chol

undertaking a success. I am grateful to Almighty God for having you all, and may He bless you abundantly.

# 1

## The Ruins of Animals' Kingdom

Once upon a time in the savanna grassland of Chakap, Upper Nile, there lived together all kinds of unruly animals (*Maluŏny*) and birds. That jungle was inhabited by all types of animals and birds of all nature before the human populations could migrate down the Nile. The lion (*Kŏr*) was the overall caretaker of all the animals in the jungle. The lion was the king of the jungle while the aquatic animals were ruled by hippopotamus (*Rŏu*) and the birds were ruled by a saddle-billed stork (*Arial-beek*).

The animals lived together in harmony as there was no animal that could eat their fellow members. Even some of them who could illegally fish were subjected to punishment before the king of the aquatic animals, the hippopotamus for a heavy fine. They used to live on gathered and collected roots and wild fruits.

Elephants (*Akŏŏn*) were in abundance. Their stubborn members would peep into the small animals' huts to check whether there were some members of the small animals inside before they could intentionally step on their domiciles. They had frequently stepped on small animals and would unintentionally step onto their houses as they passed by towards their green pastures. Thus, the small animals complained to their paramount chief, the fox (*Awan*), that the giant ones do step onto their houses and tunnels either intentionally or unintentionally!

The subject matter was reported to all the kings of all the animals, and all were summoned for a meeting. The meeting was chaired by the king of the land animals, the lion. And the agenda of the meeting was 'Exploitation and Oppression by the massive animals'. All the animals turned up for the meeting except the elephants who did not show up. The meeting was adjourned due to the absence of their chief. On seeing this, the cat (*Bura*) family members teamed up and consulted their sitting head of the jungle, the lion, for their special meeting to be conducted behind closed doors and afterwards, the outcomes of the meeting were not revealed to anyone!

The lion told them a proverb: "*Thɔn na cïe rɔt lony, ke yin col löi,*" which is translated as "*the bull will not be set free from the tie if he cannot detach himself from a cattle peg!*" And the wise saying was overheard by a cleaner, the donkey (*Akacä*). And the group of servile cats, (*Aɲɔn*) were then told to arm themselves with sharp-pointed-long sticks (*Amoth-thok*). Whenever elephants peep into their huts, they were to stab the elephants deeply in their trunks. The cats did as they were told and that scared the elephants away from coming closer to the small animals' huts or tunnels.

The elephants' trunks were swollen due to the stabbing and they went for operation at The Hares' Medical Complex (HMC). Over there at the hospital, the hares' team of surgeons immediately took the elephants to the Intensive Care Unit (ICU) where their lips were operated on and lumps of meat were chopped off from their upper lips in the operation.

The chopped off lumps of meat were boiled and taken to the patients and the staff. They avidly ate the meat and took the soup as well. They wondered what kind of roots or fruits they have eaten since all animals were vegetarians and no animal could eat their fellow animal! The donkey disclosed it to them that it was the elephants' meat that they have eaten! Unknowingly, one of the traitors, (*Dulum*) the fox, let the cat out of the bag by revealing the secret to the elephants that their members who underwent operation lost large portions of their upper lips as an intentional act by the team of the hare surgeons who later fed their patients and staffs with the chopped off meat from their lips.

The elephants went to the lion's homestead and explained to him what had happened to them during the operation. And the lion pretended to be concerned as he examined the elephants' ailing conditions. The king had to call all the animals for an impromptu meeting. And all the animals turned up for the meeting and the lion explained the whole account of what had happened to the elephants. The floor was opened for the animals to give their views, ways forward and suggestions of what should be done then.

The groups of hare surgeons were bombarded with a series of questions by the animals. And all the other animals were disappointed too during that hot argument. This invited the intervention of the sub-chief, the hare who shouted: "Keep quite please! Where is Mr. Hunger amongst you?" Afterwards, silence ruled over the meeting!

The animals' king, the lion hit the table loudly several times *Taaŋ! Taaŋ! Taaŋ!* "The meeting is over folks; truly, the hare is right, 'where is the hunger!' If you people have not seen Mr. Hunger among you, then there's no one to answer the question as to why the elephants' lips were chopped off! I hereby declare it from today onward that you can eat your fellow animal since Mr. Hunger had not turned up!"

Hmm! Wonders were witnessed within those few minutes and would never end among the animals. A cloud of dust filled the air. Things went out of control. The king himself chose and landed on a healthier cow, and apparently, the hyenas spotted goats and the cats got hold of rats. Surprisingly, the peaceful animals' kingdom turned out to be "the animal eats animal kingdom" and the animals ran away for their own safety.

At dusk, the few animals that were not eaten up ran deep into the jungle. And the law of the jungle took over. In addition, some of the birds' survivors like saddle-billed storks (*Arial-bheek*), crown cranes (*Awet*), pelicans (*Jack*) and egrets (*Ken*) found their own ways out and flew higher to the Nile swamps.

The first love and harmony between animals and birds themselves along the River Nile basin ended up in disarray after the horrible skirmish at Chakap grassland. After the collapse of the animals' kingdom, some animals and birds became carnivores, herbivores and omnivores; and this is how 'the animal eats animal concepts' began. Hence the survival of the fittest!

# 2

## Maker de Biar and the Lion

**M**r. Maker de Biar was a great pastoralist, a farmer and a hunter. He was a great leader of several Cush lands and cattle camps. His cattle camps used to move seasonally from one place to another as they searched for green pastures. In December and January, their cattle camps migrated to the Sudd swamps, toch and settled along the River Nile tributaries and marshlands. Over there, there was plenty of water and variety of green pastures which made their cattle healthier and produce good quality milk and meat.

When summer passed, the first rains (*Dëŋ-kä-Areu*) start to pour in April. And this made some farmers start to clear their farms for cultivation.

Mr. Maker Biar had rotationally been migrating from toch to the cattle camps next to their villages. Unluckily, they brought their cattle home from the swamps after a few rains had fallen, and then after, the rains stopped. Traditional rainmakers were summoned, and they could not manage to call the rain back!

At the Eastern part of the village, there was a two-days-walk-location called Gadiang; over there, there was a great deep-water point where many varieties of lions resided. Maker Biar proposed that his cattle camps must migrate to Gadiang but the people opposed him vigorously because the place was inhabited by giants that could simply eat them and their cows as well!

Maker was an influential person. He managed to change the mindsets of the aged and the youth to accept his decision by convincing them that he would fight the lions' great king over there. After everyone including his father had agreed, they proposed an immediate migration to Gadiang under a condition that Maker Biar would go and fight the lions' King.

Mr. Maker and his team members got prepared for the journey the other morning and they went ahead earlier before the cattle camps. At that time, all the lions were out of Gadiang as they had left for their hunts when the people arrived and all the lions' cubs were chased out of the area. People and the herds of cattle afterwards rushed into the water points to quench their thirst; some cows could even enter the water up to the level where they would be half-submerge and then they drink pure and clean water to their fills. The people quenched their thirst too; others could drink while dipped beneath the water.

After people and their cattle had sorted themselves out, Mr. Maker Biar instructed the youths to clear, clean and peg down their cattle pegs (Löï) at the cattle camp before the lions could return. They responded affirmatively and everything was done on time. The old men who did not have young men to peg down their cattle pegs were helped by the other youths and at around four O'clock, all the cattle were pegged down at the cattle camp.

With great surprise, the lions spotted smoke from a distance as they were returning in the evening to Gadiang where their cubs were left! And when they came closer, they could also see the herd of cattle. The lions were surprised as to who could defy the rules of the jungle to come and settle where their king puts up. The lion's king stated: "This must be Maker de Biar". The cluster of bears, duk, ogre, *ajuɔ̈ŋ* and ordinary lions arrived at the cattle camp. The youths ran to the direction where they were coming from and they lined up as Mr. Maker Biar stationed himself in front of his team members.

When the lions' king saw Mr. Maker Biar before his boys, he also came in front of his teams and asked: "Are you guys out of your minds? What made you brave enough today to come and settle here?" Uproar from the lions filled the air! Their king instructed them to be quiet. "You must be tired by now my preys. I will fight your leader and mind you please, if I defeat your leader, you will all be eaten up too and chased out of Gadiang. And if he defeats me, all my fellow lions will be killed and chased out of Gadiang as well!"

"I will give you a maximum of three days so that you guys could rest and relax before we could challenge one another for an arena fight," said the lions' king. Afterwards, the lions surrounded the cattle camp! They seriously monitored the movements of the people and their cattle within those given days so that they would not escape to their villages.

The elders fed and coached Mr. Maker Biar for two days and the other extra day was for him to clearly make up his mind about the strategies and techniques he would employ to defeat the beast (Lion's king). He was properly instructed on where, how and when to spear a lion. The tips of looking straight into the bear's eye as well as monitoring the movements of beast's legs were well stressed many times.

On the last day, the field was cleared by both the people and the lions' teams. People noticed varie-ties of lions with different colors: tawny, gold, brown and blonde. After the field was ready, the lion burst into his song:

*"Lɔ̈h tɔ̈l, lɔ̈h dië eei?*
*Wunnë aŋuam thok,*
*Wunnë anhiany thok,*
*Adhuëŋdït de raan aba wiet pïny yɔn miäk-duur,*
*Bän yuɔm de beek teem,*
*Bïe war yekɔu ya geei eei, kurum! Kurum!*
*Adhuëŋdït nɔŋ guɔ̈p ajɔ̈l,*
*Ba geet eei kurum, kurum."*

*Which is translated as:*
*"Are you entering into smoke, where are you going?*
*The team of the curve mouths,*
*The team of the awful smelly mouths,*
*I am going to wrestle you down a handsome gentleman this*
*morning,*
*And I will cut off his femur bone,*
*Of which my father will make a beanbag out of Yummy! Yummy!*
*A handsome man who is knotty,*
*I will fry him, Yummy! Yummy!"*

*After the lion's king had completed singing his song, Mr. Maker Biar*
*thundered into his song too:*

*"Adut de Nyandïe,*
*Adut nyande Wëndïe,*
*Lör toich Maker de Biar,*
*Cäm löh nhom eei,*
*Bïe wär ya yöt kenë Majöŋ-kuëi eei,*
*Makërdïe eei, töny duöh aŋoot wei,*
*Cha Kuëi liäp!"*

*Which is translated as:*
*"Adut, my daughter,*
*Adut, my granddaughter,*
*You could go to cattle camp at swamp, Maker de Biar,*
*Eat the pastures of the East Ee,*
*So that my father could jump together with Majöŋ-kuëi, his*
*stripped bull Ee,*
*My bull Maker, your swampy areas are not yet reached,*
*I assembled Kuëi, a black cow, with white forehead!"*

A panel of elders from both sides of human beings and the lions acted as adjudicators and without wasting much time, Maker de Biar dashed out into the field but was called back by both his girl-friend and the youths such that he could take with him some spears, (Täŋaröl) as well to get the tiger's skin tightened around his waist as a sign of encouragement. After he was properly armed and dressed up, he returned into the field while optimistic that he would not let the lion go un-harmed!

The lions' king roared feverishly and quickly jumped into the field. Maker de Biar was very keen in observing the movements of the lion. The lion jumped over him and he could hold his breath and stood alert holding his weapons in the beast's direction. Several times the lion tried to attack him. Throughout all the beast's challenges, Maker de Biar remained vigilant fully set on his feet.

Surprisingly, the king of the lions gave it a second thought to try wrestling as another fighting op-tion and the judges agreed, and the human beings were very happy as they knew Maker de Biar to be a good wrestler and they did not object to the idea. The lions' king claws were as sharp as razor blades and he angrily tore Mr. Maker de Biar's skin at his arms until he could jog-trot. And the lions were cheerfully clapping when their leader showed Mr. Maker some dust.

However, his father called Maker back, and the lion was doing wonders in the field as he could toss himself into the air. Unfortunately, the skirmishing teams were not aware of the proverb that: "Pride comes before a fall". Maker's father held up the injured arms of his son and spat some sali-va into the freshly torn skin. After that he sliced a cow's leather into a belt-like-straps and tied it round his son's arms to shield him from the cuts of the lion's claws. Then Maker de Biar re-turned into the field very encouraged as he breathed fire like a buffalo.

Mr. Maker grabbed the king of lions' front legs until the beast would stand like a human being on his two rear legs. And Maker pulled the lion up with its fore legs and hard-pressed his rear ones which he supported himself. The brave man threw the monster away and it de-scended with a 'thud' fall onto the ground. Again, the lion returned violently and Mr. Maker de Biar was not shaky at all. Apparently, he grabbed the lion again by its front legs and dragged him where his spears were. Luckily, he quickly picked up his spear and wrathfully cut its throat and the blood copiously poured onto his body.

The spectating human population yielded happily at the top of their voices as they could, and they dashed into the field towards the direction of the startled lions that were running away into the for-est. People overran the beasts, and the fighting went on for hours until evening when the strongest and courageous young men returned to Gadiang.

Maker de Biar was nursed at one of the temporary shelters where his wounds were washed with warm ghee. After the fighting, only three people were lost on the side of human beings and forty-three lions were killed. Maker de Biar's father was happy and contented with his son who truly took after his traits of bravery. He slaughtered his best three big bulls as an appreciation to the youth for their work well done. Many other youth also killed many more cows and every-one in Gadiang cattle camp was as happy as a king and they danced throughout the night with jubilations and ululations after they have enjoyed feasting on the cows' roasted meat. Mr. Maker de Biar was crowned as the overall leader of all the Cush land cattle camps situated along the River Nile Basin.

# 3

## Off for Exile

Exploitation, displacement and provocation between the owl (*Agumut*) and Tufted Umber or Anvilhead bird, (*adol kiriik*) a weaver bird (*Amuor*) and a dove (Guuk) and a hare (Biol) and *Atok* created a great conflict among themselves.

*Adol* is an architect by nature. It's a hardworking bird which diligently toils while building its mega nest between branches of a tall strong tree. Male and female *adol* cooperate while building their nest wherever they get married. The nest is occupied by the female as she lays her eggs while the male *Adol* goes out to look for their food.

Once the eggs are hatched into young ones, the young ones stay with their parents until they are mature and capable of being independent before they separate from their parents. That is when they would be ready to start building their own nest.

*Agumut's* nest takes time to be built since it is a lazy bird that does not make its own nest. When rains come, they just come and displace *Adol* from its nest. Whenever *agumut* approaches *Adol* at her nest, it firstly straightens its ears and opens its eyes broadly such that his ears would appear like horns as it sings its song: '*Hum! Hum! Guot cueec kwo guot cieem!*' which is translated as: "*will I pierce you at the right side or left side?*"

And when *Adol* sees its ears, it begs for a minute to pack and take out its eggs and belongings from the nest! Unluckily, the birds come to realize that *agumut* had no horns but ears when *Adol's* family members are away.

As she moved out the eggs and other personal effects, all dropped and broke accept one that remained, then *agumut* occupied the nice and spacious nest. When the rains poured, *adol* and her family members were rained on. This had been happening for a long time to many of *Adol* descendants.

One day a fox came and exposed *agumut's* secret that: 'the owl has no horns but mere ears!' The fox said that whenever *agumut* does his tricks again, *Adol* should not fear his intimidation of death threats.

Early the next morning owls came and threatened *Adol* in its newly built nest; he came and pronounced a deadly pierce at *Adol*. *Adol* was relaxed when she responded: "You can pierce me anywhere!"

The owls were surprised, and they insisted "What are you hoping for, you nut?" And the owls tried to scare *Adol* off but she did not tremble afterwards, the owl pierced *adol*, but his ears were as soft as snail, the owl was showered with shame! And every member of the *adol's* family came to know that the owl's horns were no longer horns but ears! Wonders will never end!

Many threatening birds that do not build their nests do displace the weak ones by threatening and scaring them off their nests.

A weaver bird, *amour is* also a very neat and smart bird that could wonderfully weaves its nest too. Weaver birds also underwent death threats and intimidation until recently when they could build their nests with narrow entry facing down to prevent big birds like the dove from entering to occupy their nests. Doves (Guuk) do not build their nests as weaver birds do. However, doves do build superficial nests.

In autumn and spring, it rains cats and dogs on doves as their nests are not covered at the top as weaver bird's nests are. Whenever it rains, the weaver bird asks the dove: "Has the rain stopped or has it not yet?" And the dove responded from his shallow nest: "How would I know whether it's raining or not as I'm inside my nest!"

On the other hand, the hare is also aware that the birds are easy to cheat! He designed an earthen axe and approached a bird name *Atok* that was relaxing in her best nest up a tree. The hare came and gave a warning to *Atok* that he is going to cut down the tree on which she built her nest on if she refuses to provide him with one egg. *Atok* threw down one egg for the hare to eat and he ate it quickly and left.

In the evening, the hare returned and threatened *Atok* of cutting down the tree again. *Atok* begged the hare not to do it so but he insisted until *Atok* threw at him another egg. And the hare enjoyed eating it and said: "Thank you my friend for the egg, it tastes very nice!"

Just after two days, the hare returned carrying his molded axe and he declared it as usual: "I will cut down the tree if two eggs are not thrown down for my lunch and dinner, respectively." *Atok* pleaded but it all failed on deaf ears! At last, *Atok* dropped two eggs to the hare as he had said to have two eggs dropped down for his lunch and dinner, respectively.

Both male and female *Atok* carried their few remaining eggs to an abandoned neighbor's nest to avoid the frequent disturbances from the hare. Naively, they could not tell how the hare spotted their location again. The hare spotted the new nest and approached them again while carrying his heavy earthen axe and he shouted: "I will immediately cut down the tree if an egg is not drop for me." *Atok* dropped one egg. And it was very painful for *Atok* as her eggs were getting finished and it was something incredible to lose all her eggs to the hare in such a way! She was very stressful and could not imagine what to say to the hare the next day when the day breaks.

Earlier in the morning a fox appeared while singing and passing near the tree on which *Atok* was putting up, and *Atok* immediately grabbed the chance and appealed to the fox for help as she has lost almost all her eggs to the hare. Luckily, the fox stopped and asked what the trouble was all about. *Atok* explained everything and the fox disclosed the hare's secret to *Atok* that: "What the hare carries is not a real axe but an earthen one! Hare is a liar; the hare has finished your eggs in vain! Only human being could cut down a tree but all the four-legged-animals could not do that!"

At noon, the hare drew closer to the tree while whistling and stipulated it again that he wants to slash down the tree if an egg is not dropped down for him. *Atok* kept quiet. The hare asked: "What are you hoping for comrade?"

*Atok* suggested: "Cut down the tree now and only now if you can!" The hare hesitated and insisted to bestow more warnings. But every single order and statement from the hare was violated by *Atok*, and after a while *Atok* exclaimed: "What are you waiting for pretender! I told you many times to cut down the tree, what is the matter? Continue, cut it down! Cut it down now and only now!"

Then, after the hare lifted his earthen axe and landed it onto the tree, the hare's molded axe broke into pieces! And the *Atok* family's members sarcastically laughed at the hare's deed for a long time at the top of their voices until a few birds could gather round. The hare dashed into the jungle and *Atok* related what had befallen her family. Varieties of birds learnt that an owl and the hare are good for nothing fellows and the wise were right to say: "*Meth, lɛɛr bith jieeŋ*" which is translated as: "*Child, take the spear out to the public for final touches.*"

# 4

## The Black Fox and the Hyena.

The fox and the hyena set off for cattle rustling at the lions' cattle camps. They planned how they could launch their attacks for many months as the cattle camps were inhabited by many trained monsters and ogres who had enough fighting skills.

The fox and the hyena equipped themselves with their fighting devices like clubs (*Thuor*), arrows and bows (*Madrot*). They also carried along with them some roasted meat sucked in ghee and packed in enclosed leather pouches.

They travelled for six days and on the following night, they settled beside the lions' cattle camp waiting for the dark hours of the night to clock in. Afterwards, all the cattle returned to the cattle camp. And at midnight as the fox and the hyena were sneaking stealthily into the cattle camp, the hyena prayed: "*Kuirë maa, lɔ wɔt e këdu, ku bënbei e këdië,*" which is translated as: "*Kuir, the god of my mother, entrance into the cattle camp is yours while the exit is mine.*"

Fortunately, they found all the lions asleep when they penetrated the camp. They quietly cut the plaited leather lashes, wiën which were used for tying down the cattle to their pegs one by one as they selected the best cows. They also placed the cow dung into the cattle's mouths precisely to stop them from mowing!

After all that, they moved out of the cattle camp. And when they were at the outskirts of the camp, one of the ogres woke up to answer a call of a nature. He moved out of the cattle camp and came to an open arena where he could sort himself out. Astonishingly, he spotted the cows vanishing into the woods! He yelled at the top of his voice and all the other lions were awoken and ran to the di-rection where he was yelling from. All the lions gathered within a short time, and the screaming lion was asked why he screamed, and he pointed into the forest and said: "I just saw some cows entering into the wood!"

"*Yiec! Cä löth de wär, Yördit duöt,*' which is translated as: "*Alash! How I tied a big bell of my dad, Yördit! Hurry up! Hurry up! Let's all run after them,*" said the lions' front-runner. They ran down into the jungle and it was quite dark in the woods. They had to line up in rows and ran fast in the targeted direction. After around forty minutes, the cattle came into sight. And the raiders heard the sounds made by the lions' feet as they approached. The fox instructed the hyena to chase the cattle extremely fast into the Magic Valley (MV). And he remained searching for his wooden gun, Kartuc where he had hidden it before they could go for the raid.

The lions emerged and found the fox hidden in the trees with his *Kartuc.* He gunned down one lion and quickly removed the cartridge, *akamthuur* and cocked his gun again. He then killed three lions and ran extremely fast into the valley where there was thick vegetation. The lion ran swiftly after him and he gunned down two more lions. This brought lots of panic and confusion among the lions because the fox could kill many of their members and they could not manage to distinguish him in the woods. They halted and made up their minds on their next move. One of their wise counsels advised: "It's logical and meaningful to fight the raiders immediately after dawn to spot the culprits."

They waited for three and quarter hours before the daybreak and afterwards, all the lions ran into the valley to search for the culprits, and they could not find any! They scuttled into the forests and they could not find any cow around. They then swiftly scampered into the direction where the cattle footprints were available on the muddy ground. And fortunately, they spotted the cows after two hours of their long-drawn-out search.

Then, the fox shouted to the hyena: "It's now your turn to fight the lions." The hyena waited for the angry pride of lions. However, it was a terrible fight. This was the very fight where the hyena was bitten up badly at his hind legs and he immediately became lame; he was attacked from all the direction, bitten badly on his limbs and he courageously continued to engage the lions in the battle. Regrettably, he did not pick the gun from the fox, but boldly managed to fight the beasts empty-handed.

When the fight became dreadful, the hyena narrowly escaped by running hurriedly into one of the tributaries of the River Nile. The water current carried him the same way it carried the fox and the cattle up to the Eastern plain of the jungle next to River Sobat. The hyena reached the swampy low-land where the water current was low at mega sudd swamps, *toch* where the fox and the cattle had already been. The hyena could hear the cattle mowing but, he could not see them due to the pres-ence of papyrus, *aguor*.

The hyena latterly reached the lowland as he was bleeding profuse-ly, and he was tired. He after-wards found the cattle and the fox at a distance. Since the fox is a very cunning creature; he had chopped off three quarter of the cattle's tails and he then tightly fixed them deeply into holes until the bristles could only remain over the ground. He afterwards started to scream before the hyena could arrive: "Oh! My God, the earth is swallowing our cattle! The earth is engulfing our herds of cattle! Hurry up! Come and help me pull the cattle out here please!"

The hyena came and found the fox holding a bristle of a tail of one of the cows, and he helped him pull out the said 'submerged' cow. Unfortunately, only a tail was pulled out and the fox started blaming the hyena: "Why did you abruptly pull out the tail that way; you could have pulled it out slowly to avoid an accidental breakage and cutting of cow's tail!" He continuously exclaimed and instructed the hyena:

"Let us pull the rest of the cattle out please," it happened the very first way and the fox blamed the hyena to have pulled out the cattle badly. All the tails were pulled out and the fox concluded:"The demon sent by the king of the lions has sunken the cattle beneath the ground back into his cattle camp!"The hyena innocently accepted the canny beast's statements and afterwards he left bare-handed for his home.

Later, after the hyena was nowhere to be seen, the fox turned to the direction where he had driven the cattle to and drove them to his homestead. After reaching home his wife and the children wel-comed their bread winner back home after his long search and tedious cattle raid.

After a month and half, the wounds of the cattle whose tails were chopped off healed and recov-ered and when the hyena revisited his friend, the fox, he realized that some of the cows were miss-ing tails and the hyena asked:"Why are some cows missing their tails?"The fox immediately re-sponded: "It's nature in the making; it's an aspect of hereditary, the first cow that gave birth to the other ones was rescued when the ground opened up and wanted to consume the cow that I raided from the lion's cattle camp." He continued saying that if the hyena was to come earlier by then be-fore the ground could consume all the animal, they would have saved a few of them.

A spy from the lions' cattle camp was sent to explore the where-abouts of their cattle and none was found at the hyena's home; only at the fox's home. The spy returned and delivered the information that the cattle were at the fox's homestead. After that, the fox had had a dream that the lions were planning an attack at his farmstead and he had to migrate with all the cattle to another village where human beings lived. In that village, the fox sold all his cattle to human beings and returned to his home village where he took all his children to a good private school.

# 5

---

## *Achol Of A Human and Achol Of A Lion*

Once upon a time in a land far away from home there lived Achol of a human (*Achol de Raan*) and Achol of a lion (*Achol de Kȫr*). Co-wives gave birth to their daughters both named Achol; a name given to a girl after her predecessor sibling has died or it can be a name of one's grandmother. The young ladies used to enjoy their happy times with their mums before things went sour. They used to play and walk together as they look after their cows, goats, and sheep since they did not have a brother.

After they had grown up, they moved to the cattle camp with their father. Their mothers remained in the village. Unfortunately, *Achol de Raan* lost her mother! Whenever they return home, *Achol de Raan* suffered solitude as she was used to staying with her beloved mother! Her stepmother started mistreating the poor girl and that affected her life so badly, she lost her weight and seldom played with her half-sister.

*Achol de Raan* was a very social lady; she had great sense of distinguishing between rights from wrongs while *Achol de Kȫr* was a stubborn one. At winter, they could return to the cattle camp with her half-sister and father. Their cows were fairly distributed among themselves for milk and *Achol de Raan* used to keep her prepared butter in a gourd while *Achol de Kȫr* consumed all her butter!

After three months, the young girls were summoned by their step-mother to bring home their accu-mulated butter. But *Achol de Kɔ̈r* had been consuming her ghee; she had nothing to take home. So, she resorted to cheating her parents by placing cow dung into a gourd instead of ghee.

And when they were on their way back home, *Achol de Kɔ̈r* fre-quently asked for a short rest as she had cow dung in her gourd and Achol de Raan excused her, and they rested for a while.

After their long walk and their home was near, *Achol de Kɔ̈r* re-quested again for a short period of resting as her butter was heavi-er and Achol de Raan agreed. They rested and swiftly, *Achol de Kɔ̈r* grabbed Achol de Raan's gourd and she ran home with it. She arrived home before her sister who yelled: "Why do you run away with my butter gourd?" She immediately ran into the cattle barn (luak) and told her mother: "Mum! Achol wants to grab my accumulated butter and she has cow dung in her gourd!" *Achol de Kɔ̈r*'s mother checked the gourd and confirmed that the gourd con-tained cow dung; she badly slapped the poor girl in the face and spat onto her face too.

On their way back to the cattle camp, *Achol de Kɔ̈r* transformed herself into a lion and wanted to eat Achol de Raan. But Achol de Raan begged her not to eat her:

"Why should you want to eat me my dear sister, yet I have no issue with you since?" The beast gave her a condition: "If you complain to our father about the ghee, I will eat you instantly. If you disclose what-ever you have seen to a third party, I will still eat you up. Will you?"

And Achol de Raan replied while trembling: "No, I will not re-port anything about the ghee to any-one." Finally, *Achol de Kɔ̈r* trans-formed herself back into a human being.

She did not report the case to her father after they had returned to the cattle camp; but she kept the pain to herself and the young orphan continuously suffered the mistreatment from her stepmother whenever they have returned home.

One day they were on their way taking their accumulated butter home and *Achol de Kɔ̈r* asked her stepsister: "My beloved sister, could you please assist me in carrying my heavy gourd?" The inno-cent girl agreed, and they went on their way. As usual, they rested for a while and there after *Achol de Kɔr* hurriedly walked home before her sister! After reaching home she reported that her stepsister was trying to grab her gourd of ghee!

As usual, she underwent a series of punishments from her stepmother and she wept desperately and cried bitterly. She feared to reveal the ill treatment imposed on her whenever they returned to the cattle camp. She lost more of her weight and kept on isolating herself more than before.

Luckily, her father realized that the children were having issues amongst themselves. A month lat-er, when they were taking their accumulated ghee home again, their father secretly followed them up to a point where *Achol de Kɔr* grabbed her sister's gourd and ran past her! Achol de raan then ran after her and they started to argue intensely on whom the gourd belonged to. Their father knew the distinction between the gourds and he also knew the game his elder daughter was trying to play; he knew her as a foxy girl as she consumed her ghee in his presence!

Their father brought home the quarrelling children and when the mother to the uncouth Achol heard the case; she intervened as usual and started to beat the blameless orphan desperately in the presence of her husband. Appropriately, her husband broke the ice and took the law into his own hands and started beating her stubborn daughter. His wife regretted mistreating the poor girl and there after their daughters started to live in fear of being beaten up again by their father.

When the girls were at the age of engagement, they were given the opportunity to get engaged. Achol de Raan had her humble boyfriend named Deng while *Achol de Kɔr* had her uncouth and arrogant boyfriend named Deng too; the latter wanted to snatch her poor sister's boyfriend. One day their boyfriends coincidently turned up at their home at the same time and no one was told to leave as it was late at night. They all slept in their tukul.

Overnight when everyone was asleep, *Achol de Kɔr* secretly walked out of the hut and she returned carrying a human waste on a bark of a tree. Surprisingly, she walked stealthily and placed a big portion of the excrement between her half-sister and her boyfriend and smeared a small portion at the back of her sister while they were sleeping!

It sounded like a dream when they all woke up in the morning! Achol de Raan ran outside the hut as lots of tears run down her face freely. On the second day, their two boyfriends returned at late hours of the night and they were accommodated as usual. Unfortunately, the incident happened again and that night *Achol de Kɔ̈r* stood up and complained of a horrific smell!

The well-behaved Deng gave himself a thoughtful time to clearly find a solution to this mess. *Achol de Kɔ̈r* secretly started approaching the good Deng to blackmail her stepsister, but Deng did not give in that easily! He monitored when the other Deng could visit and at that very day, the kind Deng gave it a last chance to see what used to happen with her lover! He came before the other stubborn Deng and pretended to be sick and sleepy.

And when the other Deng arrived, he conversed with his girl-friend while her half-sister did not as she was much affected by the occurrence of that shameful act in the midst of them! The pleasant Deng acted as if he was asleep as he snored.

At midnight, *Achol de Kɔ̈r* quietly walked out of the hut to bring excrement. She then placed it onto a scrap of a metal and brought it back into the room where she wanted to place it between her stepsister and her boyfriend.

The humble Deng was vigilantly watching as she sneakily approaches, he woke up and asked: "What is your motive? Why do you have to do this all along?" But she did not answer as she re-mained shocked. Everyone in the room woke up and they felt deeply sorry for what had happened. The two friends who were falsely accused rejoiced in their hearts for a quite long period of silence.

The kind-hearted Deng married his beloved wife, Achol de Raan and they were happily married while *Achol de Kɔ̈r* remained un-married. She has been hunting for a husband but did not get any responsible man to marry her. The wise men were right to say: "*Pɛl nyic yuɔm*", which is translated as: "*crafty is known by a bone*".

# 6

## Deng and His Sister Aluar

Two orphans by names Deng and Aluar struggled with their lives since their parents had passed on while they were still young. They bought two goats, a male and a female. Their goats multiplied and when they were quite many, they bought a heifer colored, Ayen.

When they were mature, they started attending their traditional dances where they were observed to be good dancers. Deng was a handsome man who danced and sang very well; he had a golden voice. His sister was an incredibly beautiful woman.

One day, his sister noticed that her brother was a good singer but lacked a crown bull for perform-ing during dances. She proposed: *"Our heifer is to be bartered with a stripped bull, Maŋaar"*. He accepted his sister's proposed agenda, and he traded his heifer with the bull.

Deng composed his many songs and ladies were all impressed with his singing styles. One day, it was his turn to look after the herds of cattle in the woods. In the woods, his crown bull turned into an ogre, ghergher. And the beast bawled: "Deng, if you don't give me your sister, Aluar, I will eat you!" Deng thought quickly and responded: "Ok, I will give her to you!"

On the fourth day, Deng's turn for looking after the cattle came and he went into the forest to look after the cattle. In the woodland, his bull *Maŋaar*, turned into an ogre; unfortunately, Deng had not communicated the quest of the ogre to his sister.

And Deng burst into a song:

*"Monytuŋ, Monytuŋ, cie wär wuɔ yiën Deng eei! Cie wär wuɔ yiën thoŋ-de-beek! Nyiir akäc-kuɔ duɔkke guup ye riɔc. Yiën Ayen weŋ-toŋdie aciennë Maŋaardie teem-nhom! Miëthke wuwac Areu, Maŋaardie ee kiu ne jɔt-yaak/ Möi, kiu apieth miɔr Yaac wär. Kiu abe diɔr laac baai."*

Which is translated as: *"Uncle Monytuŋ, uncle Monytuŋ, have our father provided us with rain hurrah? Have our father given us red-mouthed bull! My own sisters do not feel shy. In fact, my only cow, Ayen is bartered with a colorful bull, Maŋaardie! The children of my aunt, Areu, my bull mows in the summer; mow well the bull of my father Yaach. Mow until women could urinate at home."*

And the ogre sang his own song too: *"Dengdië, yi nyic yen adie?"* Meaning: *"My fellow Deng, how did you come to know me?"*

Deng returned to the cattle camp with the cattle, and he immediately informed his sister Aluar who afterwards agreed to be taken by the ogre. They traveled to the lions' farms and after two days, the ogre ordered Aluar: *"My garden is to be ploughed and I want you to collect firewood and fetch more water."* The ogre invited his fellow ogres to come and eat the poor girl after tilling the garden.

When the water had boiled, and the ogres were ready to return to the homestead, Deng's sheep prophesied the fate that was to befall Aluar. And the sheep ran up to the ogres' farms where he found Aluar and said: *"Come with me Aluar, your future here is not clear!"* They ran away ex-tremely fast and when the ogres returned into the compound, Aluar was nowhere to be seen. They went into a frantic search for Aluar.

Since the ogres have immensely powerful sense of smell; they spotted that Aluar and the sheep had run into the woods. They ran after them, Aluar was in front while the sheep followed. They ran through the jungle as the ogres sing their own song: *"Ye yin jël adi tiŋ-kaai, Aluar?"* Meaning: *"How did you escape my dear woman, Aluar?"*

Aluar also sang her song: *"Week! Week we juäc, bë dom ya puur në yɛn, ya akɔɔn, kua ya miir?"* Which is translated as: *"You, you the assembled ogres, am I to be used for ploughing the garden! Am I an elephant or a giraffe?"*

The sheep responded too by singing their own song too as they ran: *"Aluar, kɔn kɔ̈c, ba këdiënë kan luel: cɔr thiër, miŋ thiër, yɛn amän yɛn ye riŋ ne wut thok ku jal lɔ meer eei! Mee! Mee! Meee!"* Meaning, *"just wait Aluar, I want to tell you something; there are ten blind lions, ten deaf lions, I the sheep do run about at the outside of the cattle camp and plea: meer eei! Mee! Meee!"*

They ran their own way very quickly leaving the ogres behind until they reached the cattle camp. The youths saw the ogres running after Aluar and the sheep and they ran towards them. The youths rescued them and many of the lions were killed.

Eventually, Deng and her sister Aluar joyously cherished in happiness as they celebrate being to-gether again. Aluar was married to a wealthier man with many herds of cattle. And after a short time, Deng used his sister's bride price to get marry. The wise were right to say: *"Nyandu ku toic,"* which is translated as: *"Your daughter and the swamps (toic) survive you."*

# 7

## The Vulture and the Fox

A husband to the fox's sister, Mabeek lived in the Heavens and sometimes on the earth. Mabeek disappeared and emerged whenever or wherever he wanted.

One day, he and the fox planned to go cattle rustling. After they had reached the cattle camps at night, the two drank ghee mixed with milk in the gourds of the human beings. And when they were done, they selected the best cows and cut the leather cords that were used for tying them down to their pegs with their spears. As they were chasing the cows into the forest, the fox said: "Whenever I'm satisfied, I happily sing my best song!" But Mabeek warned: "Be serious in-law, what made you dare saying that?" And unexpectedly, he burst into his own song: "*Yiec! kërku-kuäu, Gwee! Gwee! Gwee!*" 'The fox's exclamation.'

Suddenly, people heard the voice of the fox as he sang and apparently, some cows started to moo in their very direction. People ran after them and when they approached, Mabeek told the fox to hold him firmly by his legs as he performed his powers of disappearing into the earth with the cows and the fox altogether! They then all emerged at Mabeek's farmhouse, and they all cherished with the fox's sister and his in-laws. At last, the fox was given his share of the raided cattle and he returned to his home.

After four days, the fox invited his friend, the vulture who then accompanied him up to his sister's home. They set off for their long journey. On their way, they arrived at a fishpond with a lot of fish in it, and luckily enough, there were many thin fishing sticks, *acïluöl*. They fished and caught many varieties of fish.

The fox asked the vulture: "Where will we get the fire from for roasting our fish?" The vulture con-fessed that he had no idea. It was sunset, and the sun's glaring beams and sparks of red rays were in sight. The fox ordered the vulture to rush to the scene to bring the fire!

He flew to bring the fire. He swiftly flew, flew and flew in pursuit of the setting sun. After a speedy long flight, he came to realize that 'It was a setting sun, but not a ball of fire instead!' When he was about to reach the sun, his eyelids and eyelashes were all caught up by the sun's blaze and got completely burnt up! He immediately changed his course and started flying back quickly to the pond as it was getting hotter and hotter over there; that's why the outline of the vulture's eyes is red.

Back at the pond, the fox had produced a fire through friction and roasted the fish among which he has selected the best ones. He ate the most excellent big fish and left a few of the smallest ones for the vulture to eat.

When the vulture returned, the fox screamed: "What has happened to your eye-lashes and eye-lids my dear?" And the vulture replied: "The huge red ball is not a fire but a setting sun! It's the very one that has burnt my eye-lids!" The vulture was given the few remaining small fish to eat. And the vulture complained: "Where are the big fish?" The fox replied: "The dog came and grabbed them and ran into the woods with them." The vulture ate a few small fish amid fox's ex-citement but it did not make any difference. In the end, the fox says: *"yïn bë cië gon yɔn cɔp akɔl nyin,"* which is translated as: *you will be like the vulture that tried to reach the sun long ago.*

Later on, the fox picked up his adeet (a light wood that is curved for both defense and storage) and spear and the vulture picked up his spear too as they continued with their journey. After hours of walking, they crossed a dried-up river where they found nice shells, thieet. They collected the best ones while on their way, but the fox suggested: "As we are going to our in-laws' home, we need not to carry simple items like shells."

Unknowingly, the fox privately placed one of his shells into his adeet and threw away the rest that were in his possession. On seeing that, the vulture imitated what the fox had done; he immediately threw away his shells as well. Afterwards, they reached their in-laws' home, and they were all welcome and accommodated. The fox went outside and told his sister to bring their food while still hot later without some spoons as they already have theirs. The food was served hot and flooded with ghee.

Immediately, the vulture asked: "Where are the spoons?" And the fox replied: "We must check our *adeet*!" The fox communicated to the vulture as he removes his shell from his adeet and he ordered the vulture to return to where he threw away his.

The vulture hurried back to bring his shells but the fox was busy eating the flooded food with ghee. When he returned, almost all the food was eaten up by the fox. The vulture returned and con-tinued to eat the fox's leftover food which had less ghee!

At the dusk, the fox and the vulture were accommodated in a cattle barn, *luak* together with some sheep and goats. The fox recom-mended: "Let's keep our spears together at the spears custody, *rïëh*." At midnight, when the vulture was sound asleep, the fox woke up and took the vulture's spear and slaughtered one of the rams with it. He skinned the ram and roasted it while the vulture was snoozing. When the roasted ram was ready, he used the vulture's spear for serving his meat. Once his mission was over, he smeared some fat around the vulture's mouth after returning the vulture's fat-coded-spear where he had kept it!

Early the following morning, the young nieces and nephews to the fox woke up and led the goats and the sheep out of luak, and they realized that one ram was missing! The case was reported to Mabeek who was afterwards infuriated after hearing the unpleasant incident. The fox's sister to-gether with her husband and the children teamed up and they approached the fox and the vulture to unearth the destiny and the whereabouts of their ram the other night.

And the fox quickly responded: "You, the family of my sister, I wish you should inspect our spears to investigate who killed the ram while the rest were sleeping at night." Everything was agreed and they hastened to where the spears were kept, surprisingly; the checkup indicated that the vulture's spears and his mouth were all smeared with fat! Alas! Mabeek asked: "What a friend is a vulture?" The fox was freed of guilt while the vulture, the scapegoat was found accountable.

The fox's in-laws badly beat up the vulture until he ran away with discoloration. The wise were right to say: "*Wunduön, cuet yïn athörbei ke yï kääc, ku wunlei cemmë jöh yï thin!*" which is translated as: *At your natives' cattle camp, you eat a premature calf while standing however, at others' cattle camp, you are bitten up by a dog.* The fox's in-laws favored him so much and they did not properly explore the logic behind the sudden loss of the ram. The vulture innocently suffered the anguish due to the fox's plot in which he was used as a scapegoat.

# 8

## The Cock on Trial

In ancient days, there was a contradiction on what the cock was all about! The animals feared him because of his trait of eating from dawn to dusk without being satisfied. Other animals claimed that he was greater than the elephant in relation to their consumption rates! The hawk also claimed to the animals that the cock could burn them up when he was discontented. They fabled about his flaming character; the cock burns those whom he has crossed with! All those rumors made the cock become isolated from the other birds.

The tiger family articulated that the cock is a god's office manager. This is shown when he crows every hour throughout the day and at the cracking of the dawn; this reflects his natural history of being a reporting mechanism to gods. Besides, the cock carries a fire on his forehead, inside its comb. The elephant also had a conflict with the cock and termed him as a proud for nothing stub-born bird.

All these arguments raised the animals' eyebrows; therefore, the elephant went to the king of the jungle, the lion, to open a case against the cock that animals feared him as their god's office manag-er, and they also claimed that he had a fire in his comb.

The lion summoned all the animals for the hearing and all the animals availed themselves except a peacock (Rumajer) who had gone to the moon for her honeymoon. After everyone had turned up, the lion welcomed all the animals and the birds and then after, he explained clearly all what he had called them for.

The lion presided over the get-together in an open field in the heart of the jungle; he opened a floor to the plaintiffs, starting with the elephant and then after, the tiger followed by putting into the picture all what they accused the cock of as an extraordinary bird who is not friendly to put up with. The elephant said: "Many of our fellow animals claimed that the cock is superior to me both in terms of my brain capacity and on the content of what I could eat compared to his. This is not ac-ceptable at all and that belief is what I disputed."

The cock was asked to tell the animals his views about the elephant's and the tiger's complaints. In a nutshell, the cock publicly declared that he was bigger than the elephant in terms of a volume of what they could consume and secondly, he denied having had any discussion with animals about who has what in terms of mental possession.

In each of the animals' bestowed chances and opportunity to air out their views concerning the ele-phant's complaints, only the hippopotamus and giraffe disputed the cock's claims. However, all the other animals suggested that whoever will be superior or inferior will be determined when the op-ponent passes the test of an eating competition where the two will be subjected to an eating excur-sion from dawn to dusk.

The donkey was sent to bring two sacks of sorghum and he swiftly brought the requested number of sacks that were poured on an open ground midst of plenty of grasses for the elephant to munch. Both the lion and his deputy, the fox supervised the competition; they instructed the aspirants that no one would rest during the eating contest which would start tomorrow as from six o' clock in the morning to six o'clock in the evening. And whoever would get satisfied earlier would be a dark horse while the other one who would continue to eat until evening would be a winner.

The contestants came earlier at quarter to six the next day and the rest of the animals arrived after-wards. At exactly six o' clock on the dot, the lion blew his whistle and the candidates kicked off to swallow as much as they could swallow. The elephant gulped chunks of grass at different rates and the cock was singly pecking the grains one by one at a regular pace.

The two were seriously watched by the lion, the fox and an African wild pig with a large head, the warthog. The consumption continued for hours and after eight hours; at two o' clock in the after-noon, the elephant got satisfied earlier while the cock was still picking his grains.

The two were called back after a long session of eating. All in all, the animals concluded that the fowl family was confirmed to be superior in terms of nonstop consumption, they owned a larger stomach. Hippopotamus and giraffe were warned that they should not judge a book by its cover.

The chair, the lion, in turn called the tiger in to explore his stance as well. The tiger said: "The cock is both a witch as well as a witch doctor; I'm the only animal that has a clock on my wall, but whenever an hour passes, a cock crows yet he does not have any watch, what makes him distin-guish times?" And on the other hand, the hawk told my wife that: 'The comb that is located on the cock's forehead is a fire which god gave him for smoldering his enemies!' And those two were the tiger's charges.

The hawk was called upon by the lions and other animals to give his accusation as per the case, but he gave an excuse that he falls short to reason properly whilst it is cloudy. More cloud in the sky showed a high potential of raining; thus, the lion postponed the hearing until the next day at nine o'clock. Certainly, it rained cats and dogs and it was a very unpleasantly cold night.

The tiger's cubs were complaining of cold weather; thus, their dad sent his two very shrewd and strong cubs to quietly go and chop off a small portion of the cock's comb while he's asleep. That was the only option where they would obtain a fire which they would use for warming themselves up. The children stealthily walked into the poultry compound and hid themselves beside the cock's domicile. While it was still raining heavily, the cubs heroically broke into the cock's quarters and forcefully grabbed a cock both at its wings and the neck and they summarily bit off a fraction of the cock's comb and quickly ran away with it. They haphazardly left the cock crying out bitterly, kaak! Kaak! Kaak!

They then returned to their farmstead and gave the portion of cock's comb to their father who af-terwards tried to light their fire, but it didn't light up at all. The tiger and his family members re-gret-tably chanted till morning. In the morning, the tiger and his fam-ily members returned for the hear-ing while carrying the chopped off portion of the cock's comb. However, the cock reported the case earlier to the animals in the courtyard and showed his puffed-up head as well.

When the trial started at half pass nine o'clock, the tiger and his family members presented the sec-tion of the cock's comb and nar-rated the whole story to the animals. The animals requested to listen to the hawk as well. Immediately when the hawk was to open his mouth, the cock crowed in the court and the hawk dropped a bomb-shell: "This cock is a witch; he has recently bewitched you when he crowed in our midst! He's calling his god so that he could send fire from the above to de-vour all of you instantaneously!"

Then the lion invited opinions and suggestions from all the ani-mals. Among the animals, the fox asked whether the cock chopped off portion of his comb was a fire or not. The lion gave it to hawk to pass it in turns to the assembled animals for viewing from side to side to ascertain whether it's ignitable or not. After it was passed among them, the assembly proved that the portion was not combustible nor was it a fire. The owl asked the hawk and the tiger to justify why they thought the cock possessed a fire and some supernatural powers for bewitching all animals when he crows whilst the hearing was on.

The hawk and the tiger failed to defend themselves at all, some of the animals and the birds' judg-ments were taken note of; they all ex-pressed disapproval of both the hawk's and the tiger's claims. After that, the leader of the birds, saddle-billed stork, *Arial-beek* and the leader of the land animals, the lion, gave their final judgments by rebuking both the tiger's and the hawk's false accusations against the cock and his family members.

They dismissed all the accusations against the cock that he's a god's office messenger, being in possession of fire in his comb and last-ly being a witch or witch doctor. The lion chiefly stated: "Both the hawk and the tiger are sentenced to two years' jail terms for false ac-cusations." And all the birds and the land animals gave their rounds of applause as they all agreed with the judgments.

When the culprits heard their verdict, they thought it was a joke. Suddenly, the animals rushed to-wards them and the two were grabbed by their legs and dragged all the way long towards the cell. On their way to the jail, the offenders refused to walk; consequently, the ani-mals properly bit them up until they could walk at a demanded pace. Regrettably, they swiftly ran into the nearby wood-lands and when all the animals ran after them, they melted into the woods and they were nowhere to be seen.

This is where the enmity between the hawk and the hen, tiger and most of medium size animals originated and persisted; whenever a hawk sees some chicks, he urinates into their eyes and picks them up. On the other hand, a tiger hides in trees, and when an animal passes by, he jumps onto it. Up to now, the two are yet to be brought to book as they are seriously being hunted by all the ani-mals. The animals said: "*Kë chak të nyic, ee thök të nyic,*" which is translated as: *Whatever you in-tentionally introduce, finishes at your known destiny.*

# 9

## The Return of Charity

A most renowned hunter by name Deng failed to kill an animal one day. He instead resorted to col-lecting some fruits and roots in the backwoods. In the evening when he was returning to his home, he decided to pass by the well to fetch some water. Unluckily, the nearby village was deserted due to a rapid insecurity after wild animal attacks. Deng did not find any means of fetching some water at the well as it was very deep.

Astoundingly, Deng heard an echo, dim reflection of a human voice from the well. He went and shouted: "Is there anyone inside the well?" A human voice was heard: "Yes, I'm inside sir, can you please pull me out of the well?" Deng replied that it was getting late since he was going ex-tremely far.

Deng left and the person inside the well cried out: "My brother, can you please pull me out of the well? I'm among the deadliest animals: a lion and a snake. I'm a blacksmith and I will give you a whole sack of spears as a token if you pull me out." Deng agreed and told him that there is no strong rope around at that very moment; he ran to one of the nearby villages that was around ten kilometers away to ask for a rope.

After reaching the village, he explained the whole story to the chief that there was a human being inside a well in the jungle. The chief exclaimed: "I will not dare go again into that jungle where many of my people have been lost!" Deng was stunned as to why the chief would talk like that, yet he's the man of the people in the village!

"Are you aware that there are spirits, *acɔɔk* over there who could communicate exactly like us, yet they are spirit?" The chief explained.

"What can we do?" Deng asked.

"I will not go there personally with you, but I will bring for you a broad-shouldered rope," said the chief. He went into his tukul which happen to be his office as well and returned carrying the wide rope.

"Go there at your own risk sir." The chief warned. Deng had no responses to his statements and he left him intoning as it was getting late.

"Hello, are you still over there?" Deng called. "Yes, my brother, I'm still over here," the person responded. Deng lowered the rope into the well and instructed him to tie the rope around his ab-domen and the shoulders as well. He did it as said and then he acknowledged Deng afterwards when he was ready for the pull.

Deng started to pull but had a very keen look before the person could come into sight to ascertain whether he's a human being or not. At last, Deng successfully pulled the person out of the well. He then untied the ropes and greeted him. They introduced themselves and they knew each other by their names and clans as well. The man went by Ayuel by name and Deng had heard his names since he was a renowned blacksmith and herbalist as well and they parted their ways.

"Do not leave please without pulling me out of the well. Have mercy on me my brother and get me out of this prison as well!" The lion howled. Deng returned and asked: "Who are you?" "I'm a lion who is stranded down here at the bottom of the well." Deng doubted and asked: "Will you not con-sume me if I pull you out?" The lion truthfully denied that and said he would not attempt doing any harm to him, instead he will give him a reward after he pulled him out.

Deng agreed and instructed him to properly tie the rope that he was lowering into the well around his belly and arms. The lion did so and notified Deng for a mega pull. He pulled the lion out of the well and the lion was very delighted. He just pulled him out of the well within a short period be-cause he was a retired wrestler and warrior, and he still had the strength. And they then parted their ways.

Deng lifted his fruits and roots and as he was on his way, he heard a thunderous call back: "Come back please! Come back please! My kind-hearted person, pull me out of the well as well please. I'm the only being that has just remained in the well." Deng returned and asked: "Who are you?" "I'm a snake," the snake replied. Deng asked: "Will you not bit me?"

The snake confessed and said: "I will not dare do that please; in return I will meet you somewhere sometime and will help you out. You even know that: '*Abïny lɔh, ku abïny bɔh,*' which is translated as: '*The principle of give and take.*'

He placed down his belongings and lowered the rope into the well. Down the well, the snake plait-ed itself around the rope and sunk his teeth into it as well so did its tail. And after a while, Deng started to pull, and the snake finally reached out and thankfully nodded its head to thank Deng for the good work as they went their seperate ways.

It was at eight o'clock in the evening when Deng reached the village where the chief gave him the rope. He found the old man eat-ing and sorry to say, the chief didn't welcome Deng even for a cup of water. Deng thanked him for giving him the rope and he replied with only one word, 'Okay!' Deng thought that the chief would ask more about the mission but he didn't. As Deng was on his way, he wondered what the chiefs of these days have become!

Deng reached home late while very tired carrying his roots and fruits. Then after, he retired to his bed and when his wife asked why he's late that day, he lied to her that he has been chasing a deer the whole day and inopportunely, he didn't manage to catch it.

On the third day, a lion emerged with a group of wild animals, *thiäŋ* and drove them towards Deng's home. When the women and the children realized that, they ran their own ways. After the lion re-alized that he had reached Deng's compound, he subsequently landed onto the best four *thiäŋ* and pulled them next to Deng's doorstep.

The cry by the women and children quickly filled the air and attracted the men who were on their hunting expedition. They all arrived as they wanted to follow the lion and luckily, Deng recalled what the lion told him three days ago and he recognized the beast as the very lion he pulled out of the well. Without wasting time, he suddenly stopped his men: "Discontinue the fight please against this lion right away! Stop aiming at him! Stop please! Why do you want to kill him, yet he has killed for us four animals?" People listened to him and they left the lion to go away unattacked. They skinned their animals and Deng divided the meat among their households. They didn't go for the hunt for the next two days.

The blacksmith, Ayuel didn't think of fulfilling his promise. Deng had to go up to his home and after recognizing that Deng was the one who pulled him out of the well, he was almost dead of embarrassment. He paradoxically welcomed Deng and tried to cover up his fault by telling him many baseless stories. One of them was about how the raiders terrorized the whole of his village.

After they have conversed, Deng reminded him that the scorching sun was approaching, and it was his time to return home. Ayuel made a clean breast that his spears were collected by raiders during the latest village invasion. He gave Deng a he goat and he claimed that his promise holds some wa-ter. Ayuel escorted Deng up to the juncture where they bid each other a goodbye and his previous friend went on his way with his goat.

Ayuel took a different route altogether towards the paramount chief's home immediately after they separated with Deng. And he found the paramount chief outside his tukul. And Ayuel greeted: "I greet you my supreme chief," And the Paramount Chief replied: "I greet you back too," and he welcome him for a seat. After a while, the paramount chief asked: "How can I help you? Are your subjects all doing well?" Then Ayuel said: "Yes, all is fine, but someone is moving away with my goat. He's moving towards the well". "Messengers! Messengers! Messengers!" The paramount chief called his messengers to come, and they all showed up within a minute: "Go very fast right now towards the well and you will find a person leading away a he goat from our village, bring him and the goat all to me." And the messengers dashed out.

The messengers went as quickly as lightning. "Hey! Stop! Stop!" One of the messengers shouted at Deng who then pretended to have not heard their call. "Hey! Hey! The one who is leading away a he goat, we are with you; Stop! Stop!" The messengers continued. After they were together, one of the messengers told Deng that they were sent by the paramount chief to come and take him to-gether with the goat to his compound.

Over there in the compound, Deng hesitated and asked a reason as why the paramount wanted him. Without answering, Deng was savagely beaten up and was taken to the cell where he suffered star-vation and dehydration. Overnight, the very snake that he pulled out of the well appeared from un-known direction and woke his friend, Deng up and he asked: "Did you pull out any snake out of a well sometimes back?" And Deng replied: "Yes, I did." And the snake updated Deng: "Okay, I told you last time that I will meet you somewhere anytime and will help you out of a problem. And as immediately as I leave from here, I will go straight away and coil myself around the beloved wife to the paramount chief and mind you, I will not harm her. In wrapping up, when you hear people puzzled, tell them that I'm your object of worship and the lady will be brought before you in substitute of Ayuel."

Earlier in the morning when the paramount chief's wife was busy cleaning the compound, the snake made slow progress towards the wife and tossed itself onto the women and coiled itself around her belly. A cry of agony was heard by everyone in the nearby villag-es. "Wonders shall never end," cried the messengers. The paramount chief collapsed and remained seated in his armed chair with his mouth wide open. All the messengers were in confusion as to what to do next! Oth-ers were proposing immediate shooting while others were demanding immediate cutting.

"That snake needs me; it's one of the subjects of my divine animals; have the cell opened and tell the lady to walk into the cell," Deng explained. The cell was unlocked and the lady came in carry-ing the snake around her belly. Over there, Deng requested: "For this lady to be freed, call in Ayuel, the one who falsely accused me of a theft." And the messengers instructed Ayuel to go in-side the cell: "Come here Ayuel!" And when Ayuel heard that, he took to his feet and the messen-gers caught him within a few seconds.

Surprisingly, Ayuel cried out loudly: "No! No! The gentleman whom I accused of theft is not a thief; I only accused him falsely." The paramount chief opened his mouth for the first time: "Since the snake has coined itself around the tummy of my dear wife, do whatever Deng tells you, my people." Deng shouted: "The paramount chief's wife is being squeezed badly at her abdomen, I told you before to bring Ayuel over here into the cell!" And then Ayuel was pushed into the cell by all the paramount chief's messengers and as immediately as he entered the cell, the snake unfas-tened its ties and sprang onto him and he was bitten several times to death.

Deng caught the terrorized paramount chief's wife by hand and led her out of the cell. "Mine, mine, welcome back honey," said the paramount chief as he hugged his cherished one. After that, the para-mount chief instructed his soldiers to let Deng go on his way without any questioning. At last, Deng thanked his snake for the rescue.

He left the goat at the paramount chief's residence and went on his way. Over there, Deng reached his village, and he was welcomed with both hands opened. And Ayuel's body was found lying on the floor of the cell but the snake was nowhere to be seen.

# 10

## Why the Bat Prefers Upside Down Posture

I n the ancient kingdom of the birds and the animals, there existed an extraordinarily strong relation-ship and bond between different varieties of living things. All the animals lived in harmony with each other as they reproduced in good health. They recognized the moon together with her children, the stars as their friendly provider of light at night. The myths put it across that the sun is barren, but no one had some rituals for her purification, so that she could make a replica like moon as well. The animals were so confused on how they would help their master provider of light and warmth, the sun in return. The animals called for a conference where the entire animals' and the birds' king-doms converged in an open and wide lowlands of Dung-Abiei.

They were informed and after all the animals have arrived, the king of the jungle, the lion stood up and said: "I greet you and we all feel affection for each other and we are always bound by the prin-ciples and the ideas of our age; we have all gathered here to give some positive thoughts and ideas on 'what we could give to the sun in return for her being generous and kind enough in providing us with both light and warmth.'"

The animals and the birds affirmed that the sun is very crucial for all the living things' continued existence and thus, she deserves to be acknowledged for her nice works well done. The floor was opened for the animals to air out their ideas one by one.

The cow said: "In view of the fact, we, the animals and birds repro-duce offspring, but the sun does not; why couldn't we carry out some rituals, in the names of cleansing her so that she could pro-duce her young ones as well?"

The animals put their hands together: "Yes, if we are producing, why doesn't our ancient fellow reproduce too?" The animals and the birds unanimously agreed that they were to carry out some cleansing and rituals for the sun to reproduce.

A flying nocturnal mammal, the bat, keenly gave it some fair thoughts on what could happen if the sun acquire her offerings: "If one sun could heat up the universe, what if they were as many as the children of the moon, the stars?" Silence ruled over the animals' and the birds' get-together as they were making up their minds on the credibility of the bat's idea.

The elephant highly praised him by saying: "The bat's contribu-tion is logical and carries material facts. Yes, we may get burned up if the sun produces her children." The birds and the animals held up the bat's opinion.

The sun was eavesdropping on the animals' and the birds' debate. Consequently, she lowered her distance and badly heated up the uni-verse. The sun said: "You, the bat, do not ever look at me, oth-erwise, you will die." From that very day up to date, the bat does look at the sun as he was told to adopt an upward down posture instead. This is the genesis of enmity that exists between the sun and the bat.

# 11

### The Adventure in Luak

I n the month of September, in the land of Jieeng, there lived a
hunter by the name of Machuor. He hunted alone along Mïny
permanent water-land, *toic*.

As he was returning home from the cattle camp, he was badly
rained on by a pronged heavy rain. While he was walking in a cold
weather, a deserted *luak* came into sight and he rushed towards it for a
shelter. After he had entered the luak, there was no one residing inside
it, other than a monster that was hiding in its darker parts as he waited
for his roasting head of a human being in a heap of burning cow dung;
a fire source in the middle of luak's bonfire! Machuor drew near the
fire and sat adjacent to the lion as he warms himself.

However, at one of the darkest corners of luak; there waits a lion
whose claws were as sturdy as a claw hammer. However, Machuor did
not recognize the presence of the beast at the other side of luak. After
the lion, saw the man settled, he went towards him quietly and said:
"Excuse me please, I want to remove my roasted meat here!"

The man patiently waited to find out the kind of meat that was being removed by the monster. Sur-prisingly, the monster dug into the
fire with his claws, and he finally removed a roasted head of a human

being! The man was puzzled as the monster slaps lightly his roasted human head to clean it from some burned cow dung ashes. What the hunter witnessed by himself was like a movie, and the adventure was like a dream!

The hunter got the idea of running out of luak immediately; he took to his feet and quickly loped out of luak. No sooner did the lion saw Machuor dashing out of luak than he swiftly ran after him with a deer's speed. They both ran pass a savannah land and then through a thick and lastly to a dense forest. After a long period of a chase, the lion stopped and deafeningly said: *"Aa yïn bië ber lɔ luaŋ tuekkë ë nhom de raan thïn!"* Which is translated as: *Will you ever dare enter a cattle barn where a human's head is being roasted!*

The man ran fast the shady wooded area without looking back to affirm whether the lion was still chasing him or not and eventually came into view at the rural community plains where he met his fellow villagers herding herds of cattle. The herders told him to rest before they could ask him what the matter was.

After he had rested for a while, he regained his strength and reluctantly narrated everything he has encountered as he returned with the herders to their home village. And eventually, his colleagues said: *"Wëi atö në Nhialic,"* which is translated as: *Life is from God.*

# 12

## Achol: The Elephant

Long, long time ago in the land of Monyjang, there was a severe famine that swept away a half of the lives of the animal's population; the few animals that had remained after the great flood sub-dued the land died of a severe starvation. The aftermath of that mammoth hunger lingered into an abrupt changing of a widow called Achol into an elephant!

The poor woman gave birth immediately when the people returned to their empty homes after the end of the great flood. Achol's simple tukul was located at the periphery of the village. She gave birth to a baby boy but she had no food to eat. She stayed inside her tukul for weeks as she silently starved and after a prolonged period of persistence, she was tempted to roast her newborn boy. And whenever she wanted to place the infant into the fire; the child laughed. And Achol mono-logued: "Alas! Mine, mine, my innocent boy, will I really roast you alive?" She tried many times to throw the baby into the fire, but the love for her young boy put her into a dilemma and eventually, her predicament helped her survive the little poor baby.

During the famine, things turned out from bad to worse; Achol held her child in her arms and walked out of her unfilled house. She went to a nearby tree where she plucked leaves and ate them. She did that from tree to tree until she vanished into the woods. After she was satisfied; she looked for a water point where she could quench her thirst.

In the process of picking and eating the leaves for several months, she gradually transformed into an elephant. Her nose developed to be a long-drawn-out extension which revolutionized into an arm and her lower canines grew into horns. Her plodding transformations happened under the very watch of hunters and the gatherers.

Without any doubt, she finally developed, transformed, evolved and changed over to an elephant! In comparison, the elephant eats and cries like human being. Its udder and vulva resemble that of a human being and when an elephant is killed, the young men are not allowed to turn up when its meat is being detached. If the merciless famine had not swept across the rural village, the poor Achol would have not turned into an elephant! Poverty is unjust, when it befalls a human being; it transforms them into a deadly beast of dissimilar character altogether.

# 13

---

## The Betrayal at Upcountry

I mmediately after the creation, the dog and his cousin the fox were putting up at human beings' residence. At the end of the winter season, the cattle camps started to migrate into marshy water lands, toic where the pastoralists would put up until the summer ended. The dog moved simultane-ously with the travelling herders, but the fox stayed behind in the village.

The dog and the pastoralists reached the cattle camp of Padim-aduët lately in the evening and sub-sequently they cleared up the vicinity before they could hit down their cattle's pegs. Over there, there was plenty of pasture for their cows to produce sufficient milk. On the other hand, many gen-tlemen culturally killed a lot of cows (*riöŋ*) in the name of their youth hood pursuit of life-time recognition, self-importance and pleasure.

The dog solely had the advantage of collecting lots of fleshy bones, stillbirth calves and afterbirth; the fox wrote a letter to the dog that he wanted to come to the cattle camp as well. The dog was not happy with the request by the fox. He knew that the fox was slippery, and he could outwit him if he comes to the cattle camp. He personally went on his way home and told the fox to come with him to the cattle camp after they have had their forged consultative talks.

They ambled for hours before they could reach the cattle camp. And over there in the camp, it was promising to rain, in fact clouds were always pregnant; consequently, the dog went to the nearby heap of dry cow dung and dug into it a shallow tunnel where he could position a fox when it rains. It by then started to drizzle and before it could rain heavily, the dog dashed to his neighborhood and stole a buffalo's hide which was used for covering the twin boys to the chairperson of cattle camp (bänywut). The father to the children searched for his leather and it was nowhere to be found.

The twins immediately started to cry out sharply as it seriously continued to rain on them, his father made a wide-ranging inquiry, but he did not find it. He could hear his children weeping as well; he then decided to return to his locality. On his way, he spotted his hide stretched over a mountain of cow dung. He quickly rushed and removed the leather on top of the fox. "You, the little fox, how dare you? Is it courage to stealing my twins' leather?"

"Gweeeh! Gweeeh! Gweeeh! I'm a visitor to the dog, *Atuliet*, *Baak-Atuŋtin*, I didn't steal the leath-er from you; it was brought to me by the dog," the fox shrieked as he was imperfectly beaten up by the leader of the cattle camp. The fox darted into the forest and the dog ran after him. The owner of the leather took his and covered up his young kids who were being rained on.

Over there as they were chasing each other in the woods, the dog and the fox had a second con-structive talk and consequently, the fox agreed to return to the cattle camp. As they get nearer to the cattle camp, several bulls concurrently bellowed at the top of their voices, which confused the fox. "What is happening to the bulls?" The fox asked. "It's all the uncastrated bulls who are vigorously bellowing to express their prime of life." the dog explained.

When they were few meters away from the cattle camp, a bull bellowed again, and the fox en-quired: "Why did a bull singly bellow instead of the mainstream this time?" "It's being castrated!" The dog said. "No! No! 'This cattle camp where men straighten fishing spears at their chests will fall apart one day!' Sorry to say my cousin, we are immediately parting ways; each one of us will solely be putting up at his own locality! And mind you, where someone would get comfort and a piece of mind is more fundamental than being enslaved." The fox explained as the dog was shed-ding crocodile tears.

"Okay, go well cousin and take care!" The dog said. The fox hur-riedly ran into the forest and the dog at a snail's pace returned to the cattle camp. Currently, the dog is coolly putting up with men while his fellow dog family members: wolf, jackal, fox and the coyote are inhabitants of the back-woods.

The dog became a friend to both human beings and the cows and at whatever time people have milked their cows, they give the dog his share of the milk. Following the regular rains of May and June, the cattle camps returned to their villages. And at home, the cattle enjoyed pleasant immature plenty of green grass and in return, the cows pro-duced lots of milk. The people and the dog en-joyed better, cordial and healthy friendship at their home.

One day, the dog went into the woods to visit his cousin, the fox and the fox proposed a stiff jumping completion over a cattle barn (luak) between the animals that feed on grass, the herbivores and those that feed on flesh, the carnivores. The dog seconded the idea and he opted to pass the information when he returned to the village as the fox informed the wild ones. As soon as the dog reached home, he passed the information to the chair of herbivores, the cow. Both the herbivores and the carnivores agreed to partake in the competition in two days' time.

On that great day, both group of carnivores and the herbivores gathered before luak. The elephant was their renowned referee. The best carnivore high jumpers, the cheetah and the lion were nomi-na-ted to open the show from the carnivores' side while the best herbi-vore high jumpers, the cow, the goat and the sheep were the second after them. The carnivores' candidates passed the test; they made it simply to jump over the luak without any difficulty.

But, when the cow, the goat and the sheep had their turn, they had terrible falls with thuds onto the ground. And they all lost their upper

teeth in the process and when the dog saw that incident; he had a prolonged laughter! And in the process of expressing his amusement, his
mouth had an in-stance cut by splitting and widening at its corners;
that's why a dog has a gashed mouth.

# 14

## Lion: The Leading Reign

Before the hippopotamus came to a decision of living both in water and on land, he initially used to live on land like other land animals. His lifestyle transformed when a wildfire spread with a great speed consuming almost all living things inhabiting that locality. In that fire devastation, hippopot-amus got seriously burnt; it was burnt up when passing through a blazing fire and its fur wholly caught fire in the process, and his appendages, ears and the tails got seriously burnt. Only his red-skin-membrane was left exposed! The victim reported home latein the evening while completely burnt. When his two lovely nephews: the lion and the hyena saw their maternal uncle burnt badly from head to toe, their hearts were broken, and they burst into tears.

Their uncle, the hippopotamus said: "Nephews, crying is not the solution of serving my life; take me to one of the deepest water bodies." "The deepest water sources are located far away uncle," the hyena commented. "No! No! Cousin, we must take him though the deepest water bodies are as far as the sun," the lion suggested.

The lion arranged their travel to kick off immediately that evening, instead of travelling during a sunny day. They travelled the whole night non-stop until it dawned, good to say, they were then far away from their home. The hippopotamus burnt body was re-exposed to the heat from the sun and that made their travel in the sun the next day more hectic compared to their unruffled travel the pre-vious night.

At dusk, the hippopotamus thoughtfully tried to get up again to walk at his last night's regular pace, but his body got swollen more due to the burn and it pained him a lot. But he tried by hook and crook to keep his steady strides. Fortunately, his strides started to widen in the earlier hours of that morning. Their journey was fastest at night and worsened during daytime.

At around midday, the hyena felt the kicks of hunger and he had to yell at the top of his voice as they hadn't eaten for the periods they had been travelling. The hyena began to salivate after seeing the choc-olate-like-burnt-body of his uncle and to make thing worse, some of the blisters started to burst and this sharpened his appetite.

The hyena put it forward: "Cousin, our uncle is a gigantic animal; if we could eat some part of his body and lead him to the water bodies, I would like that!" "That's an abomination cousin! How can we dare eat our own uncle, it will never ever happen when I'm still alive?" The lion strongly con-demned the hyena's idea. As they walked for a while, the hyena repeated his very statement, and the lion gave it a deaf ear.

Unhappily, the hyena jumped onto the neck of the hippopotamus and hungrily grabbed large pieces of flesh at his neck. Without any delay, the lion reacted by responding to his act appropriately and he escaped with foremost injuries. The hyena went ahead via bushes and hid himself in the grasses beside the path before he could launch another attack. And when the lion and the hippopotamus were near, the hyena aimed at the hippopotamus' right ear and quickly chopped it off before the lion could act, and again, he swiftly dashed into the woods. After he had eaten his meat, he again went ahead and hid at the left edging of the path where he launched another assault of seiz-ing his left ear yet again; he for a second time took off with it.

The lion had a merciful watch over his much-loved uncle as he bled profusely and, he encouraged him to walk as fast as possible. He took courage and trekked along the way as recommended by the lion. After a while, the hyena stealthily followed them through the bushy hedges and hopped onto the back of hippopotamus where he bit off his tail and ran back into the woods. He enjoyed the chopped off tail. The lion kept himself under a careful surveillance as he quickly led his uncle to the water source.

The hyena did not come back until the lion led his uncle to the river. "Here's the deeper waterside uncle," the lion said, "Try to jump into it to ascertain whether it's deeper or shallower!" He jumped into the waterside; deep to the bottom of the waterbed, measured its circumference, and emerged. It was fantastic; it portrayed a sense of permanent water availability. The hippopotamus recognized the importance of his being led to the water source, overwhelmingly; he was greatly impressed and thanked God for the kind help from his nephew.

The hippopotamus finally concluded: "How blessed are you, the lion, from today onward, you will possess a strong sense of smell for confusing your preys; you will luckily be hitting your food-stuffs at a mere bare ground like a playing-ground and an ignorant individual, the hyena will eat nothing." The lion was blessed to attain his meals without much struggling while the hyena was cursed of too much laboring when seeking his daily meal. The hyena depends on leftovers, car-casses of dead animals and on old woody substances.

After all, the hippopotamus burst into his own blessing song:

*"Ba weŋ ya yɔk te ɣer wiu, te ɣer pak, te cië riaŋ de Paloc, wën ghëi rɔt abë dak cam!*
*Mënh cɔl kör, Mënh col yɔr, meth apel nyin, leer nërë tony thiäŋ, tɔny ye nërë lɔ bot piny, na tul ee ke lɔh yöc,*
*Raak weŋ ke jol ka mɛnh de nyänkäi aah, ba weŋ ya yɔk te ɣer wiu, te ɣer pak, te cië riaŋ de lɔr, wën ghëi rɔt abë dak cam!"*

*Which means: You will find a cow just at a clearer ground, at a bare ground of Paloc field where people dance, and an ignorant fellow, the hyena will eat nothing!*

*A child called the lion, a child called the lion, a child is schem-
ing; he took his uncle to a deeper water body, where his uncle
submerges, and when he emerges, he bounces.
Alas! You will milk an expecting cow my nephew! You will find a
cow at just a clearer ground, at just a bare ground like dancing
field where people dance, and an ignorant fellow, the hyena will
eat nothing!*

And at last, the hippopotamus appreciated and blessed the lion for
the job well done and he in-structed him to go on his way. Just within
few days, the hippopotamus recovered and became a thick-skinned-
semi-aquatic mammal which lives both on terrestrial land as well as
in water. His bitten off ears and the tail remained shorter; they did not
grow longer and his burnt skin color turned out to be dark-tanned.

# 15

## The White Lie

Long, long ago before the Stone Age, beasts and monsters were more populous than human be-ings. And people lacked suitable means of farming and for killing deadly animals. Woods and carved stones were their deadly weapons. It recently became a different story altogether after the introduction of weapons and tools through technological advancement which led to specialization of human population that was then divided into two groups of agro-pastoralists and fishermen.

Agro-pastoralists used to live at home as they looked after their cattle and farms. The villages were located closer to each other for convenient fortification. On the other hand, fishermen dwelt at per-manent swampy areas, *toic*. Frequent visitation to the villages was avoided; they rarely visited each other because of the prevailing fear of man-eaters on their way between the villages and toic.

They used to move in groups whenever they were travelling back home. Many persistent attacks on the way by both the birds, people, flying and prowling monsters were imminent and the point of path divergence (*apok-kuer*) was where many cases of men-eating incidents happened as witnessed by the few lucky survivors along that path either on their way to the rural community or on their way to toic.

A black bird with a long beak, *Agaal* was one of the victims along that route.

*Agaal* recently fled that deadly route, and he immediately had a vow of becoming a dumb after hearing from his neighbor a white lie about a sudden death of his mother! He crossed over from toic to the village a few days ago, through the dangerous forest to take his mother some fish.

And after he had taken them, he returned to toic where his neighbor lately returned from the village and lied to him that 'his mother is dead because of starvation!' And he asked his neighbor: "What about the few fish that I recently took home for her?" And the lying neighbor replied: "They are all over!" And at last, Agaal vowed: "If that is the case, I swear not to speak again from that day henceforth!" He instantly became a dumb with an immediate effect from that very day up to date; he does not speak, even to utter a single word!

One day, a man by the name Wadeh decided to cross from toic to the village, he did not fear the monsters at all on the way after making up his mind that lying to the man-eaters on the way would revive him. Secondly, the old man had many children whom he could leave behind in case he was eaten up by the monsters on the way. He went on plaiting a typical grass whose strands were inter-laced and woven, arieeh to make a big basket, akook; basketwork designed up to a human being's height.

Akook was used for storing farm output but Wadeh designed it for a camouflage purposes as he wanted to cross over to the village through the monster infested forest to home, so only small holes were left open for him to see.

He started his journey earlier in the morning and around noon time; he reached *apoh-kuɛɛr,* where the monsters waylay the human population. The monsters were very confused, and one of them asked: *"Where on the earth does akook walk like a human being! Akook noŋic ŋo!* Which is translated as: *Akook, what is inside you?"*

The monsters gathered alongside the path as they innocently watched the big basket moving. Little did, they know that the old man was inside it! The chairman of the monsters asked: "*Akook*, where are you going?" It was something of mystery when the monsters heard *akook* replying: "I'm going somewhere! Do you have another question to ask?"

The monsters were stirred up by the phenomenon: "It is very strange, how can an akook speak like a human being?" The chair of the monsters gave it a fair thought at last by asking his members: "If we eat this *akook*, we will eat an evil, and if we let it go, then it will be a mistake for letting our foodstuff go like that. What shall we do?" The monsters did not give an answer as they were all confused and in a dilemma as they followed the strange akook moving until the village was near.

The villagers saw the monsters approaching and they blew their horns and beat drums for their ur-gent gathering. Luckily, the beasts ran away when they saw the youth coming as they blew their horns and beat the drums.

The old man came alone into sight and the villagers ran towards the moving akook and one of the brave men asked: "Who is inside this *akook*? Are you a human being or a ghost? And if you are a human being, tell us your names and your clan." The man told them his names and his clan, and they all recognized him. The people approached him and opened his akook, and inside akook were some fresh and dried fish for his fellow villagers.

The villagers were astonished and praised the old man for his intelligent thought as they recalled the wise saying 'What can be seen by an old man while seated cannot be seen by a child while standing.' At last, the paramount chief said: "You are an icon, Wadeh! This cross-over through the monstrous jungle between *toic* and the village was an incredible legacy mission," the villages' par-amount chief affirmed Wadeh as one of their cleverest and the bravest elder of his terrain.

# 16

## The Enemy from Within

A young man by name Chanbet and his sister Ayak set their feet to a marshy vicinity where they could efficiently and effectively collect some roots. Chanbet had a fear that the area was inhabited by many ogres and monsters. When Chanbet and his sister were engaged in the collection of roots, time passed by and they were late.

Chanbet requested of his sister: "Please Ayak, we are late; why don't we leave by now?" And Ayak said: "I have not yet collected some roots for my grandmother, grandfather, aunt, uncle." Chanbet waited, waited and waited for his sister Ayak, but she didn't respond to his brother's re-quest.

Afterwards, Chanbet left for home but his sister remained until sunset when monsters found her over there at the water source. The ogre arrived and asked her:

*"Ye ŋa cit nyin Ayak? Ayak nyankënnë de ŋa? Ayak nyankënnë de Chanbet. Cïe Chanbet lɔ tën-no? Chanbet acïe riŋ roor kennë läi kɔ̈k.*

*Cuɔ̈lkë nyïn cïë we amok! Ku yakke kɔc len ye kɔc läät? Dhuɔ̈ldë abɔ cïën abäkkë bën luel ye kë ye we kɔc läät!"*

Which is translated as: *Who is this who resembles Ayak? Whose sister is Ayak? Ayak is a sister to Chanbet. Where has Chanbet gone to? Chanbet has run into the forest with other animals.*

*Your eyes are as black as your earth holes! Are you guys solely here to abuse others? Many more are following us; you will tell them why you just abuse people!*

The monsters got hold of Ayak and took her to their locality where all kinds of animals resided near a big water point. And over there, the fox secretly told Ayak: "Find your way out up the tree please!" And afterwards, Ayak climbed the tree as she was told to do so. And all the animals then gathered around the tree where they slept after they have cooked and ate their food.

Overnight, she was informed by the fox to climb down the tree when all the animals were sound slept; and she descended stealthily by stepping onto the biggest animals: elephants, hippopotamus, buffalos and followed by other animals as she descended from the tree.

After she was out of the zone; she was taken to her parental home by the black fox. And the fox was much appreciated and thanked for the work well done. Her relatives were very delighted, and they slaughtered a goat for him as a sign of appreciating him for bringing back home their lost daughter.

The goat was cooked and brought before him. He ate a portion of the meat and when he was satis-fied, he carried the remnants back where he left his fellow animals. He returned very slowly and quietly and moved where the hyena and *thiäŋ* were sleeping. He nuzzled and smeared some fat and meat around the hyena's nose. After he has completed his plot, he dropped some chunks of meat and bones randomly around the hyena and marched towards *thiäŋ*; he also painted *thiäŋ's* body by passing a sooty saucepan around the back parts of its body before he dropped it onto the ground.

Earlier in the morning, the animals came to realize that Ayak was missing, and they were surprised as to how she managed to escape in the middle of the entire animals' family. The chief ogre asked: "Where is Ayak?" The black fox quickly gave his point: "Someone among us has eaten the poor girl! Hei, look at the hyena's mouth, and *thiäŋ's* body. What's strange and special about how they look?"

Astonishingly, there were many chunks of meat and bones on the floor and animals were upset as their eyes were fixed on the suspects. Both the hyena and *thiäŋ* had no room for arguments as the animals were very annoyed. The animals could not control their anger; they geared up their reaction and rushed towards the two suspects and they held them firmly and they asked questions. In con-trary, the two yelled at the top of their voices begging the animals for forgiveness but the animals offered them deaf ears instead.

Commotion filled the air as the animals' empire was in turmoil: "Quiet! Orders please! Keep the orders," the elephant shouted. "What will we do to you as a punishment; instead of killing the two of you?" All the animals requested answers from the suspects before they could take laws into their own hands.

It was a hot debate whether the two animals would be killed or not; and at last many animals pro-posed that they should not be killed. Consequently, *thiäŋ* was then given a permanent sooty mark at his back and its horns were curved backward while the hyena was made lame! After the animals, had dealt with the accused ones, they sent them out of the empire as they were taken in as pitiless and ruthless fellows. Up to today, hyena walks with difficulty because of the injury inflicted on him by the animals at his limps. And *thiäŋ's* horns were curved backward and it also has black marks as a sign of his being beaten up.

Over the years, a dog let the cat out of the bag that the girl that was held hostage by the animals is currently with human beings; she has narrated more about animals' kingdoms secrets. She said that she was rescued by being returned to her parental home by the black fox! When the animals heard that information, they were all upset for dealing badly on the innocent hyena and *thiäŋ*. They then hunted for the black fox which escaped instantly after the incident and vanished into the woods and the dog ran to the man's residence.

The animals which seriously took part in beating *thiäŋ* and hyena regretted a lot and they blamed themselves for having not examined the material facts critically in the disappearance of the poor girl, Ayak. And the elephant concluded: "A suspect should be held free and innocent until proven guilty."

# 17

## *Not A Man Enough*

Long, long ago before the animal kingdom could get transformed by developing civilization roots, humans and animals were very wild, but animals feared themselves more than human beings and a few courageous animals had intermarriages with humans. And only the powerful beings ruled over the less powerful ones. Legal ownership of property did not exist; animals were used to taking chances by grabbing whatever they liked at a time and place as theirs.

*Raan de Raan,* which is translated as a *person of a person* met a beautiful and hardworking young girl named Awut, who was well brought up by her stepmother. She was a naïve and a respectful young lady. Even the animals knew that she was a responsible and industrious girl; she could wake up at five o'clock and clean their compound, grind sorghum and millet and cook porridge. And lat-er then in the late morning, she would fetch water.

The monkey applied for an admission of engaging her and he was the first to be acknowledged. He couldn't hide his happiness! Afterwards, the fox applied, and he was not admitted. These two small animals lived next to human residents and they had interest in marrying Awut. It annoyed the fox most that he was not allowed to date the most beautiful and hardworking lady. He approached the lady during his fine days and tried to convince her.

The fox set his feet into the human cave where the girl and her relatives were staying and tried to defame the monkey; he met the beautiful one behind closed doors in the absence of her parents. And luckily, he had enough time with her in which he corrupted the lady's mind by feeding her with his truth and facts which favored and lifted him higher and lowered his opponent, the mon-key.

The fox damaged the monkey's reputation by revealing his physical appearance to be of enough ugliness to lower the monkey's dignity.

He said: *Munyduɔnnë, ee mony rɛɛc athar-jany-nyäny, Munyduɔnnë, ee emony rɛɛc anyin ŋonon, Munyduɔnnë, ee emony rɛɛc col cin, Munyduɔnnë ee emony rɛɛc ayɔl wärrät!*

Which is translated: *Your husband to be has flat buttocks, your husband to be has sunken eyes, your husband to be has dark hands and your husband to be has a very elongated tail.*

The lady was easily convinced and gave in as per what she heard. Afterwards, the fox left for his home after spending enough time brainwashing the girl. And when the monkey paid a visit to his in-laws' home, his fiancée was not welcoming at all! The monkey was confused as to what had happened to their relationship! The monkey asked her fiancée: "Why do you look gloomy today honey? What's wrong? Have I wronged you in anyway?" The lady replied: "I'm okay and there's nothing that is wrong with me. What shows that I'm gloomy? And did I tell you that there is some-thing wrong with me?"

Since monkey is a smart primate; he immediately made a diagnosis that an unfamiliar person has propagated some seeds of humiliation on his way. He tuned up his conversation to be catching and con-structive with his girlfriend until she could open up and speak out. It caused monkey a much more time to dig out the undisclosed utter-ance that has caused havoc and disorder between his companion and himself. And finally, she revealed what the fox said: "Your husband to has flat but-tocks, your husband to has sunken eyes, your husband to has dark hands and your husband to has a very elongated tail."

The monkey exclaimed: "This indictment is not a serious matter to break our relationship apart!" He continued to explain what made him look the way he looks these days: *Kë jäny yen thar, ee rëër në thöc-yic, ku ke göl yen nyin, ee chiëŋ de mandeer, kë col yen cin, aye piu ke galam ku ke yiën yen thar yöl; cïn raan de we cïe kon kueth ne dɛu? Ee yol de dan de weŋdie!*

Which is translated: *What flattens my buttocks is prolonged sitting on a chair, what sinks my eyes is a protracted wearing of eyeglasses, what darkens my hands is the ink of a pen and why I have a tail; don't anyone of you have many calves? What I have is a tail of a calf of my cow!*

Awut was convinced and realized that the fox was a blackmailer; without any causation, she re-sumed her relationship with the monkey. And the monkey planned to officially marry Awut who afterwards approved his demand.

One day, the two marched out of the cave and walked further towards the jungle where the two accidently met Awut's father returning home; and the old man was dissatisfied with her daughter's fiancé.

As the two were emerging into the woods, Awut's father emerged from the wood and asked where the two were going: "Where are you going Awut? What have you become of these days my chil-dren? What's special about your relationship?" And Awut responded: "He's my husband to be dad!" And her father growled: "Your husband to be! If I'm your dad, then, why wouldn't you lis-ten to my statements? Your marriage will never ever happen this way if I am still alive!" Yieech! Is this a procedural marriage approach by a well-brought-up gentleman?"

Awut's father asked: "You monkey, are you ready to marry my daughter?" The old man moved towards the monkey as he positioned his heavy fighting club (*thuɔ̈ɔr*) at his right hand! The mon-key then did not risk waiting for the fuming man who afterwards threw his *thuɔ̈ɔr* at him. Luckily, the monkey dodged it and ran away swift-ly onto a tree. And again, the old man speared the fleeing monkey but missed him as he hurriedly ran away. The monkey fled away and climbed tall trees where he swung from tree to tree leaving the old man cut off. Awut's father said: "You are not a man enough; if you were, you would have waited for a fight!"

# 18

## The Inter-Worlds Marriage

The drumming fellows did their best by beating the drum rhythmically; the dancers majestically danced, sang their ancestral songs, chants as the dust filled the air. The better you dance, the more you are recognized and appreciated by others. One of the best dancers, Deng was also endowed with a golden voice.

In the process of dancing, an ostrich feather landed on Deng's head and it got stuck in his designed hair (*aŋuet*). The crowd admired the feather as it was a glittery one; tall and colorful. Surprisingly, he didn't know whether there was a feather that has landed on his head or not! And when the dances were over; young men escorted their girlfriends, and even Deng walked with his too. His accompanied girl appreciated his feather as a nice and lovely one, and in contrary; Deng checked his head and found that there was a feather on his head. Deng replied: "Thank you my dear for appreciating my feather."

Deng did not then participate in their talks with the girl as he was trying to figure out when or who put a feather on his head. He tried to figure out who gave him the feather, but it was all in vain. He went to the cattle camp and proceeded to his *dhien*, one's vicinity where cattle are kept. Deng was quite disillusioned as he could not remember someone putting a feather on his head; besides, he only begged a simple dancing feather from his friends, but they didn't have extra ones. After all these, Deng said: "This is something of mystery!" He again tried to gather his thoughts day and night, but he could not remember anything at all.

He handed overlooking his cattle to his next of kin as he returned to the village and as he was ready to start his journey back home, he removed the feather and placed it into *aruɔl*, hallow-bamboo-like-flora and carried the feather to the village where he kept it in their hut. Deng didn't tell his mother all that had happened in the cattle camp while he was dancing.

After some few hours, later, Deng informed his mother that he wanted to return to the cattle camp after he had placed his feather in a safe corner within their tukul. Deng's mother was flabbergasted why his son brought back his dancing feather to the village and left earlier to the cattle camp! He didn't give a convincing reason, but he left concealing the occurrence.

Deng's mother used to look after some few cows that were left behind for the young ones to feed on, so no one usually remained at home and whenever Deng's mother went out to the fields to look after the cattle, the feather turned into an incredibly beautiful lady! And the strange lady took over the household responsibilities; she did whatever task a woman performed; she pounded and ground grains and at last, she cooked.

Whenever the old woman returned, she found well-cooked food. When she asked her neighbors whether anyone had cooked for her, they said no! It happened in the fullness of time. One day, the old lady decided to lay a trap of seizing the doer; the one who cooked at her homestead in her ab-sence.

One day, Deng's mother hid herself besides her hut at ayälic, an extension of the hut until at around mid-day when the strange girl appeared and had a glance around but, did not see anyone around. She had some serious glances once again but there was no one around. After all, these in-spections, she started her household tasks, pounding millet, grinding it, and eventually cooking the family meal.

After all the activities were completed, the girl was in her rush of returning into the room but Deng's mother emerged from her hiding and held her firmly in the process. And when she realized she was seized, she turned into a snake, but the old woman did not let it go. Then she transformed into soil, but she still held her determinedly. And thirdly, she turned into water, but she still held it. After all these changes, she changed into herself, a beautiful young girl at last.

The old woman appreciated her: "Thank you for seeing you in yourself once again!" And Deng's mother asked her: "Who are you and where did you come from? And can you please tell me more about yourself; your lineage/roots, clan and family!" And the strange lady replied: "I'm the feather your son, Deng brought home from the cattle camp and even if I tell you who I'm and where I came from, you will not understand it!" And the strange girl finally disclosed herself: "I'm from another world, far indeed! And I'm by name: Anok Garang Deng, from the clan of Deng."

"I have never ever heard of such a clan!" The old woman confessed, "But we will still find it out when my fellow village men come." The two had a nice conversation in the old woman's very lan-guage. And in the evening, the girl refused to eat; and the old woman was confused of what to do next. At last, she decided to pass a message asking her son to return home from the cattle camp; and the message was then passed along.

After a day, Deng came from the cattle camp. And no sooner did Deng arrive at the village than the old men gathered at the old woman's compound and the talks were chaired by one of an elder who afterwards asked the girl: "Can we please know you by names and your ancestral background?" The strange girl stated: "Even if I tell you who I'm and my ancestral roots, you will not understand it! I'm the feather that landed on your son, Deng while he was dancing at the cattle camp a month ago! I'm from a different world, far away from here! And my names are: Anok Garang Deng; from the clan of Deng."

An elder asked: "How will we get in touch with your parents?" The strange girl answered: "If Deng agrees to marry me, I will only go with him to my home if he wouldn't mind!" And Deng gave his remarks: "I have fallen in love with her, and I will go with her to her parents' home." Their deal was over, they had to visit her parents first and then they would work on their marriage processes if all went well.

On the second day, Anok declared their journey and said to Deng: "Hold me by the legs; we get to fly to our world," After a long flight, they came to a mighty gate into a beautiful and wonderful mega city in that world. The gate was opened for them and they were led to their city. Over there at home she had to pass him to her closest relatives at their homes before she could proceed to her own parental home.

*"Ye monydu ëkënnë Anok?" Thïc wëlënnë. Ku dhuk Anok: "Emonydïe wälën, ye näk yen, ke näk, ye päl yen, ke päl. Deng, ëken ya lëk yiën wän ye panda arεεc luk thïn waa!"*

*"Ye monydu ëkënnë Anok?" Thïc weiyïe. Ku dhuk Anok: "Emonydïë wuwac, ye näk yen, ke näk, ye päl yen, ke päl. Deng yekën ya lëk yin wän ye panda arεεc luk thïn waa!"*

*"Ye monydu ëkënnë Anok?" Thïc kueere. Ku dhuk Anok: "Emonydie kukuar, ye näk yen, ke näk, ye päl yen, ke päl. Deng ëkën ya lëk yin wän ye panda arεεc luk thïn waa!"*

Which is translated as: *"Is this your husband Anok?" Her uncle asked. Anok replied: "Yes, he's my husband uncle, if you want to kill him, kill him and if you want to leave him, leave him. Deng, didn't I tell you that the judgment is worse at our home!"*

*"Is this your husband Anok?" Her aunt asked. Anok replied: "Yes, he's my husband aunty, if you want to kill him, kill him and if you want to leave him, leave him. Deng, didn't I tell you that the judgement is worse at our home!"*

*"Is this your husband Anok?" Her grandfather asked. Anok replied: "Yes, he's my husband grandfather, if you want to kill him, kill him and if you want to leave him, leave him. Deng, didn't I tell you that the judgment is worse at our home!"*

And many more relatives later asked her.

After she had passed most of her relatives, she eventually reached her own family home where she was happily welcomed by her parents with her earthly husband-to-be, and they were allocated a room with her husband. After she has met most of his in-laws, Deng invited them for a marriage to be conducted on earth. That's where in-laws would collect their dowry.

An elder put across. "Don't worry in-law, we all know your relatives as well as your ancestry tree; they are very responsible ones. We will go for our bridal wealth; secondly, what matters is a love between you, young people!" Their travel back to the earth was scheduled to be in two days' time. And when the moment in time came, they started their journey earlier in the morning to the earth.

Deng was told to hold his fiancée by legs as they start their journey back to the earth. A return journey was faster and easier than going to that world. After sometimes, they landed on Earth es-pecially at Deng's compound. Deng's mother welcomed the in-laws: "I salute you all my in-laws and I welcome you to my home and urge you to feel at home."

"Go and inform our village elders for an urgent meeting in thirty minutes' time at my compound," Deng's uncle passed a message to one of Deng's cousins. All of them were informed and they made it to the meeting point on time. The chief, his colleagues and the in-laws gave their greetings remarks before the marriage negotiations could begin: "We, the clan of Chieeng'dit welcome you in the names of our ancestors. We all apologize for being late since you were seated."

After their introductory remarks, the clan chief explained: "Our son has fallen in love with your daughter, and we all cherish and thank you for hosting him. And for the today gathering, we are going to bind a relationship between our clans." The marriage negotiations went on well and it smoothly proceeded; Deng's family presented a total of seventy-seven heads of cattle while his pa-ternal and maternal uncles paid a total of thirty-nine heads of cattle. The total number of heads of cattle paid as dowry was one hundred and sixteen.

The heads of cattle that the bridegroom's family paid were only meant for the bride family and both bridegrooms' paternal and ma-ternal uncles paid their shares of heads of cattle to the bride's paternal and maternal uncles as well. Deng's in-laws were overwhelmed by their reception; Deng relatives' willingness in releasing many heads of cattle impressed Anok's relatives. The marriage negotia-tions did not last for long time.

Afterwards, the bride price negotiations were concluded with blessings and bindings of the mar-riage by the two bargaining par-ties by slaughtering bulls separately. Deng's relatives slaughtered two bulls as a marriage seal to the Anok's relatives and on the other hand, Anok's relatives ordered three bulls too from their world and they slaughtered them for Deng's relatives as a marriage seal.

As members from both sides were enjoying themselves with the bulls' meat, thundering voices of ululating groups of girls who were bringing their beloved sister, Anok to her home were heard. It sur-prised Deng's relatives so much when they heard people descending from above singing songs. The bride and her friends were seated after they have sung their marriage songs. The bridegroom's family slaugh-tered a third bull for the girls.

When the marriage proceedings were successfully completed, the bound clans were gathered out-side an open field for the cleansing of the couples. And after the purification of the couple, Anok's relatives together with their heads of cattle were escorted into an open area where they allowed Deng's relatives to return home. No sooner did the Deng's relatives go for a distance than Anok's relatives and their herds of cattle were simultaneously seen ascending into the skies. That inter-worlds marriage overwhelmed all the villagers.

# 19

## The Hyena's Testimony

After human civilization had taken its itinerary, a wildlife conservation act was then passed. Ani-mals' protection laws were enacted, modified and applied afterwards to shield game parks and game reserves. However, jungle laws were previously in control in the Stone Age where every an-imal was for himself and the might made right either to kill or be killed or eat and be eaten!

In the woods, there survived two cousins: the hyena and the fox together with their families, they were the only inhabitants of the Ruup Jungle. The hyenas' descendants were very ruthless as they depended so much on their neighborhood domesticated animals: goats, sheep and cows. One day, one of the hyena's children fell sick and his sickness became serious. The hyena was brought down to earth by the deadly sickness of his child.

During this time, the fox came and told the hyena that he needed to pray so that his child could be set free from the dreadful evil attack. He loudly started to pray at the top of his voice to God for a heavenly intervention: "I do not yearn for other belongings; I don't covet human being's animals: a flock of sheep, a trip of goats and a herd of cattle that come my way. I don't touch others' posses-sions! What else have I done my God to let my only child go like that? Leave him alone please; no one owes me anything even a needle!"

A fox immediately shouted: "You mean you don't long for other's movable belongings? What a prayer cousin! Yiec! The child will possibly pass on if that is all about your prayers. How will your God serve your dear child if you are not that sincere to him; open up yourself and the child will be rescued from the mysterious fate?"

"Yes, my brother; I only seized and ate one goat that was passing next to my homestead some days back; that's the only offence I have ever made since my childhood," the hyena confessed. "You are almost to the point cousin; you are not that far from the truth. Did you gain your weight from the very goat you grabbed? Try to recall on all the offences and atrocities you have made!" The fox suggested.

"I'm very apologetic my God to have not confessed and apologized willingly; I'm sorry and ask for a forgiveness for the wrong I have done my God!" The hyena confessed to the mighty being. Fortunately, he was forgiven, and his child recovered immediately from the sickness.

One of a sensible monkeys once said: *Raan ye riɔc në Duciëk ee ŋiëc piër, ku yennë kee tän de mië-thke eya!* Which is translated as: *A person, who fears the creator, lives a prosperous life and so do his/her offspring.*

# 20

## *Man Alone*

Once upon a time, an infertility disaster struck the fox neighborhoods. One day, Mr. Fox was in-formed that his mother could not have kids any longer.

Instead of lamenting the fate of not having a brother, he rejoiced with a smile. 'It's not a big deal folks if my mother becomes infertile after she has brought me forth.'

Days later, Mr Fox was found answering a call of a nature by the roadside. With such an act con-sidered as immature and childish, Mr. Fox was later asked the reason as to why he did such an embarrassing thing in a broad daylight. With shame written all over his face, he responded: 'it's be-cause I lack a brother who should advise me of what to do and what not to do!'

# 21

## *The Wise Judge*

One tale that concerned child abduction was heard when a tiger took a calf and claimed it to be his. And that case was difficult to be settled. The animals sat down one day to settle the case of the child custody. In a real sense, the animals feared the tiger, they knew he was not right to keep the calf in his custody, but before ruling him out, they consulted the fox. And then the fox heard from each side of the case and he asked them to return for the ruling the following day at lunch time.

When the animals turned up for the meeting the other day, the fox appeared in no hurry to give his opinion. Instead, he bathed in a large mud puddle. Then he cried as if he was overwhelmed with grief. The animals were mystified and asked him to explain what was wrong with him. He replied, "My father-in-law died while giving birth!"

The tiger finally interrupted the talk with disgust: "Why do you listen to such rubbish? We all know a man cannot give birth. Only a woman has that ability. A man's relationship to a child is dif-ferent."

Then the fox immediately replied, "Aha! Then, you have no right to claim the ownership of the calf as you did not determine your re-lationship with the child. The custody should be with the cow." And the tiger was unsatisfied but the other animals all cherished the fox for his wise ruling.

# 22

## Baak-atuŋtil, The Powerful Dog.

The lions had been eating many people for a long period of time in many African savanna villages. And people resorted to staying together in their ancient villages. Many lives were lost especially in a wide-open-field between their villages and the lions' densely populated forest.

Luckily, *Baak-Atuŋtil*, a powerful bright dog and his kid took the venture of protecting their friends, the human populations from being eaten by lions; they inhabited a wide-opened field where the lions used to eat people. *Baak-Atuŋtil* and his kid were feared by all the villagers because of their gargantuan appearances.

Their presence between the villages and the forest was of a great security concern as most of the lions were discontinued from attacking the villages. The two dogs severally invaded the lions in-stead in their dens and caves.

Three cousins, Deng-Chiek, Deng-Baar and Madit decided to go for a courtship at a faraway vil-lage. They collected their food stuffs and went for the journey. Both Deng-Chiek and Madit would some-times change into lions whereas Deng-Baar did not. Madit was a close friend to Deng-Baar and whenever Deng-Chiek proposes eating him, he refused.

They reached the village where they were going for courtship and settled at Deng-Baar's sister's homestead; his sister was married to a monster. And in that compound the young girls were ab-ducted from shantytowns by the lions. The young men liked the girls and they dropped their agen-da of befriending them.

The gentlemen proposed engaging the girls and afterwards, they proposed their elopement as well and the girls innocently agreed. On their way, the gentlemen ran short of their food as they were return-ing home with their girlfriends and consequently, they declared eating them instead.

Madit and Deng-Chiek ate their wives while Deng-Baar did not. He ran away swiftly from them with his wife as they left his man-eat-ing cousins busy ingesting their friends.

No sooner did Deng-Baar separated from his carnivorous cousins than other monsters joined them, and they hungrily ate their girl-friends. Just within a short time, the monsters completed eating their victims and suddenly ran after Deng-Baar and his wife. Luckily, they reached the field where *Baak-Atuŋtil* and his kid were.

*Baak-Atuŋtil* and his kid furiously fought the monsters and rescued the couple. "Thank you *Baak-Atuŋtil* and your kid for rescuing us," Deng-Baar expressed his thankfulness as they were escorted to their home by the dog.

At sun set it became very dark and many mosquitoes took advan-tage. And on the other hand, the cool weather threatened them so much, forcing them to shelter under one isolated cattle barn, luak. Surprisingly, many indigenous cows and polled cattle (chot-chot) were found wandering unattend-ed in luak!

The dogs did not know that the hornless cows were monsters. And lately in the night, they fero-ciously attacked *Baak-Atuŋtil* and his kid. And on a defensive side, the dogs stood their ground, and they gallant-ly challenged the monsters until they could run out of the cattle barn and they left behind their herd of cattle.

"Round up the cattle and let us continue going on our own way," *Baak-Atuŋtil* gave orders to the team. They walked the whole night and earlier in the morning, they reached Deng-Baar's village. And *Baak-Atuɲtil* said: "You guys can now go in peace; there is no more harm here." Deng and his wife gave some congratulatory remarks at last to the dogs for their help as they drove their cattle home. *Baak-Atuɲtil* and his kid became the villagers' powerful police-dogs.

# 23

## The Squirrel and The Elephant

Before human being could become renowned farmers, wild animals used to farm better than humans and they cultivated diverse crops. Squirrel, *alɔl* was one of the best animals that had many farms in the past despite it being a rodent. It had farms where he planted vegetable and fruits with his wife and children.

One day, *alɔl* went for a hunt and his wife remained at home. Unsuspectingly, the elephants came grazing besides his garden and it continued to graze until it reached the mid of the garden and they destroyed all the fruits and vegetable.

And when *alɔl* returned in the evening from hunting, he found his garden devastated and all fruits and vegetables were lying vulnerably on the ground. He was very sad, and he asked his wife aggressively: "Who did this dirty deed in the garden? Was it mankind with his cattle or someone else?" "It was neither a mankind with his cattle nor other small animal; they were elephants," his wife answered him with cowardice in her voice.

*Alɔl* was very sorry, and he said, "It was because I wasn't here, otherwise I would have taught those elephants lessons that they would never forget in their lifetimes." The wife was puzzled, and she said to squirrel: "Your testicles will mislead you *wun mithkie,* the father to my children!"

# 24

---

## *The Broken Promise*

I t's of a cultural heritage that any intended marriage is bound to parents' approval. A young man named Chan was in love with three different girls. And when it was his time to marry, he tabled the girls before his father. And his father called his immediate relatives and explained to them what he has heard from his son.

During their investigations and analysis on which he should marry, his relatives found it out that each of the three girls had an issue to talk about. The first girl was accused of theft, the second one was alleged to be promiscuous and the third one was said to be stubborn. The immediate family members agreed that their son should marry the stubborn girlfriend instead of the other ones. It was afterwards the right time for the relatives of the son to approach the family of the girl to inform them about the marriage suggestions and to set standings and bonds of their affiliations.

The bridegroom's relatives were accepted, and the marriage proceedings were scheduled for the negotiation of bride prices, and after reaching their deals, they happily went on with their marriage ceremony and finally, the bridegroom officially took his wife. The couples were happily married and after a decade, they had three boys. Among the boys, one passed on. The family had a donkey that they used to pull a cart for their commercial benefits. One day, the father to the boys drove the donkey up to the town seventeen miles far away.

The cart was full of different goods which were bought over there, and it was very heavy for the donkey to pull it until home. In the evening, the donkey refused to pull it at all and suddenly laid down when it was almost to reach home. It absolutely refused to stand up although it was bitten severely. The man left the donkey lying down and proceeded home carrying some of the load.

"Good evening," the man greeted. "Good evening too," his wife responded. "The donkey has just laid down and refused to stand up near our home," the man explained, "This needs us to go togeth-er and help reduce its load." "It has become very useless donkey now-adays, I must have to kill it today," the wife strongly expressed her opinion. "Is that the reason you want to kill the donkey; you should not think like that please," the husband exclaimed.

"Let us just go to the site and you will just witness it right away by yourself!" She thundered as she walked out of the house, followed the path that led to the town. They afterwards reached the site and found the donkey still lying down. In a second, the wife speedily pulled out a double-edged steel sword that she had hidden in her dress and heartlessly hit the donkey at *ŋuik*, the be-hind section which links the neck and the head.

"What have you done my dear? Are you out of your mind?" The hus-band asked her as he quiv-ered. The donkey only had a few kicks before it died, and the wife rushed towards her husband and hit him at his left arm with the sword. "Help please! Help! Who can help me out please?" The man yelled at the top of his voice as his wife severely hit him.

The husband kicked her in the arms while lying down and the sword fell, and he got hold of it and unsympathetically chopped off her head. "This's not me at all! Who has messed us up?" The man cried out loudly and ran for hours to his old-aged father to inform him about what has happened. His father came with him to the site, and they met and agreed to throw the corpse of his wife into the nearby old well be-fore it dawned. Early in the morning, they lied to the villagers that his wife was carried away and eaten up by a pack of hyena.

After a funeral, the man arranged to marry a second wife to take full control of his household tasks. His marriage was then completed within a month and after a year they were blessed with twin boys. "It's my time to die and I only need the presence of my beloved son in this house," and after his son has come, the old man requested other members of the family to get out of the house.

And they all quietly marched out as the old man whispered to his son: "Do not please tell anyone what happened between you and your first wife and where we threw her. Do you promise that you will not disclose it to anyone?" "Yes, my father, I will not disclose this information to anyone come rain, come sunshine," his son responded. "Thank you, my son, for your promise," and the old man appreciated him and passed on immediately.

Since then, his second wife has been asking him frequently what his father told him and he refused to disclose what the two men talked about. This issue created a rift between the man and his new wife who complained that his husband does not trust her. One night, she asked her husband: "Did we not agree that we have become one flesh since the time we became husband and wife, if so, why don't you trust me? Am I not your wife?"

The husband murmured and at last, and he started to narrate the entire incident of what happened between him and his first wife and what they did then with his father as well as all what they dis-cussed with his father before he died.

One day, when she was cross with her husband, she disclosed everything that she knows about the death of her husband's first wife. All those who were around heard the information and the news quickly circulated until it reached the relatives of the deceased and that immediately triggered a heavy inter-clan fighting that night and her husband, children and stepchildren were all killed. She remained alone in the compound and only tears freely rolls down her checks and the people utter: *"Muɔr ee tik, rɛc käke, cɔlke kälai,"* which is translated as: *a bullock woman destroys her stuff, thinking they were not hers.*

# 25

## The Disheartening Appointment of an Owl

L ong time ago, birds convened to elect the leader that would represent them in the general animals' meeting. Birds' issues were not always considered as they lacked representatives. During the meet-ing to nominate their leader, the guinea fowl was the first speaker who described the saddle billed stork, *arialbhek* as an intelligent, beautiful, and a tall bird who could be elected as their leader.

The room remained silent and the owl kept his eyes rolling in dismay and he bewitched the guinea fowl's head making him became bald instantly.

Subsequently, the vulture seconded the guinea fowl's idea and he also went bald in the same man-ner.

Marabou stork, *dheel* stood up gently and he proposed the arialbeek as a good-looking, smart and charismatic leader who could represent them in the general animals' con-ference and absurdly his hair vanished too.

The crane, *Awet* grabbed the chance and explained to the gather-ing: "Many of us who had nomi-nated the leaders of their choice have instantly lost their hair; why shouldn't we choose a leader like owl? I nominate the owl to be our leader for this term."

The owl was very excited, and he said: "You have wisely chosen the leader of your choice; thus, you deserve to have your hair." The crane did not lose even a single hair and it remained beautiful up to today!

The birds did not wish to nominate the owl as their leader, but because of his magic, the birds opt-ed to nominate him unwillingly. If birds see an owl passing by, they keep on bullying him even today!

# 26

## *Like Owl, Like Owlet*

After a long period, an owl called his son and gave him a permission to marry as he had reached a marriageable and mature age. The owl's descendants are the ugliest of all the birds; so the owl told his son to marry a daughter of a saddle billed stork so that their family would have genes to have some beautiful children. The owl believed that if his son marries into a beautiful family, his son will get a chance to produce stunning children.

The owlet struggled to meet the daughter of a saddle billed stork. One day, he met her in one of the festival rites where the owlet waylaid her and inadvertently conversed with her for a long time. In their meeting, the owlet eventually communicated his love for her and declared his proposal to mar-ry her. And finally, after tough talks, the saddle billed stork daughter agreed and gave him the go-ahead to consult her elder sisters and other relatives.

It was then the right time for an owl and his relatives to approach the family of the saddle billed storks to inform them about their proposed marriage meeting date for negotiating bridal prices, and the setting of terms and linkages for their relationship.

When the owl together with his son reached the house of the stork, they were heartily welcomed and given traditional hospitality as they were holding deferential messages. The owl and his kins-men bravely stood behind their son. "Thank you folks for welcoming us into your premises. We came here today to inform you that our clan men wish to have a relationship with you by having the daughter of the saddle billed stork to be part of us through a marriage; especially to my elder son," the owl spoke with his eyes rolling like baseballs. However, the negotiations went on for hours.

At the end, the saddle billed storks' relatives accepted their marriage proposal and they booked a date where the two parties should come together to negotiate the bridal prices. Thereafter, the pay-ment of bride price would be done on the same day. The owls returned with their other relatives after the crucial function.

At their agreed time, both sides of the bride and the bridegroom came together for the marriage ne-gotiations; payment of bridal prices and carrying out of other marriage ceremonies. And all went on smoothly as planned. After the negotiation, the bride prices were handed over to the in-laws and the ceremony continued in pleasure and contentment on the second day. In the end, the owlet was given his wife and they all went home with happiness and joy.

Four months after their marriage, the owlet's wife was returned to her parents' home after she con-ceived as the culture and traditions dictated until she delivered. After her delivery, the message was passed to the owl and his relatives. It was vital for them to visit their newborn baby straightaway.

There was an extremely high expectation from the owlet as well as from his father to see the physi-cal resemblance of the newborn baby. When the owl and his relatives came to see their child, they dubiously found a child that looked like them, but did not look like the beautiful saddle billed stork. Eventually, the owlet's father said: "My son, we will never ever be helped out!

# 27

### The Hyena on a Test

Once upon a time in the land of wild cats, there lived a giant hyena. The giant hyena survived the deadly pack of wolves' bubonic plague that claimed many lives in the animals' kingdoms in the jungles. Since then, the hyena offspring have been lame. Before this could pass down to his de-scendants , the giant hyena complained a lot about his being lame to the deity as he was disadvan-taged when chasing his prey for his continued existence.

The deity was more concerned about his complaint and he decided to meet the hyena face to face for a direct talk before he could be healed. During their get-together meeting, the divine being as-sured the hyena that his limbs' strength would be restored if he would pass the test of crossing three rivers flowing with blood, variety of lumps of meat and thick soup without swallowing any of it, otherwise, his deformity would not be fixed!

The hyena assured the supreme deity as he alluded to one of the tests he passed: "Many years back, I passed a hard test when I proposed to marry a daughter to a human being; imagine, I was told to sleep together with a healthier puppy in the same hut however, I did not harm him until daybreak; I only carried it around and leaked his back though I was very hungry. That was how I managed to marry a daughter to the human being. This test of crossing the rivers flowing with blood, soup full of chunks of meat would just be a simple test!"

The hyena trekked to the first river flowing with cow dung mixed up with blood and luckily, his appetite was not aroused. He managed to cross it effectively without any hesitation. Afterwards, he reached the second river flowing with blood with tributaries flowing with nice soup with a few meats; he also crossed them successfully.

After a while, he arrived at the third river flowing with a good-looking soup and chunks of meat in arrays; however, he couldn't manage to let it go at all as he did not want to miss the chance! Over there, he started to swallow much of the meat and took some soup and said: *"Kä ke wëntok, le riem ke nyin wei!"* Which is translated as: *for the only son's possessions, blood uncontrollably flows away!* The hyena hungrily and impatiently took the pleasure of gulfing the meat and took the soup despite the assurance of restoring his haste and walkabout in his venture!

After eating much of the meat, the hyena arrived late at the scene where he was to meet with the deity. However, the deity challenged him for breaking the promise and eating the contents of the third river he crossed. Consequently, the hyena failed the test. Surprisingly, he walked away and preferred being a lame rather than restoring his muscle fitness! He ran back to the three rivers and found them all dried up! From that ancient time, up till now, the hyenas remain lame.

# 28

## Help Him Out

One day, a leopard sat down sobbing bitterly beside a pool of water. A young boy collecting water for their calves at a nearby cattle camp saw the lamenting leopard and he asked: "Why are you cry-ing? You are one of the mightiest beasts of the savanna lands."

"I'm much starved," the leopard said. "I have hunted for days now and have not caught a thing. The animals always see me approaching and afterwards, they run away."

The boy, feeling sorry for the young leopard, promised to meet him the next day. "I will help you!" The boy exclaimed.

The next day, the leopard waited by the pool of water and the boy came bounding toward him car-rying a small bucket and a brush. "How will a bucket and a brush help me out of this hunger?" the leopard asked.

"Wait for a while and you will see it. Now sit still and I paint you," he said. The boy sat beside the leopard and painted small spots all over his skin. He motioned the leopard to the pool of water, and when the leopard looked at his reflections, he grasped and cried: "What good will spots do me?"

Now, you can creep and hide in the tall grasses and you will blend into the shadows. The animals will no longer see you coming," the boy said.

Just before dusk, the leopard sat patiently at the edge of a small patch of grass as the herd of zebra was making their way across the plains. The leopard leapt and, to his surprise, he caught one. The spots had worked! The leopard would no longer be hungry.

# 29

## The Dogma of Give and Take

Once upon a time, a young hunter went on a hunt together with his dog. Deep in the forest, the hunter saw a monitor lizard, agaany; he called his dog and said *"ber, cam ku durɔc,"* which is translated as: *come, catch and bite it but do not fear.*

The dog refused to attack the reptile and the hunter hurriedly ran after agaany chasing it seriously. After a long chase, agaany counteracted in self-defense and it quickly coiled itself around the hunter's legs and wrestled him down!

And he yelled at the top of his voice: *"Help! Help! Ber jɔh, ber jɔh, cam ku durɔc!"* But the dog turned down the hunter's call for help and the hunter assured the dog that he would not provide him with the reptile's meat later if it is killed.

It was not that easy, the hunter seized agaany by its tail and bit its tail severely and it immediately uncoiled itself around his legs and the hunter managed to kill it and brought it home.

After the reptile was perfectly cooked, the hunter consumed all its meat without any sympathy to give even the cleared bones to his eyeing dog! And he finally said, "Tit for tat is sometimes a fair game! Did I not ask you for help when I was wrestling with the reptile and you declined to act ac-cordingly? It was a matter of give and take my pet!"

In the end, the hunter managed to execute his promise that he would not provide the dog with any meat for declining to rescue him when he was wrestling with the monitor lizard.

# 30

*The Irresponsible Wife*

A man was living with his ill-starred wife at their residence in the countryside, but their relationship was sour. His wife failed to do her household tasks; she didn't not cook at home even at times when there was plenty of food to be cooked!

On a fine day, her husband went on a fishing expedition. Over there at a *toic, a* marshy region, he killed a big fish and punched a hole in the fish's lower jaw and fixed a rope to carry the giant fish.

And when he came near his homestead, he recalled how horrible his relationship was with his wife and unfortunately, he threw away the fish and came home empty-handed!

# 31

## United You Stand, Divided You Fall

Long, long ago in one of the rural villages, there lived an old man with his ten sons. He was old to the extent that he could not manage to do light work but his sons kept on fighting among themselves and there was no one among them who would work in the household. He was very worried and concerned about how he could unite them. Their family became extremely poor and they could not even manage to afford a meal and when his father saw that he was full of regret.

One fine day, he called all of them to his bed and requested his elder son to go and bring a bundle of ten sticks. He brought them as directed by his dad. Their father ordered his elder son to break the tighten sticks while they were bound together in a bundle, but he could not manage. He told him to give the bundle to the second elder son, but he could not manage it either. They all tried their best in that order up to the youngest one, but they all failed to break the sticks in the bundle.

The old man intervened and told the eldest son to untie the bundle of sticks and gave each one of his brothers a stick and in surprise, each one of them simply broke his stick. And at last, their father concluded: "My sons, if you are united, no one could defeat you and if you are divided, you will definitely not withstand the works of the opponents." After saying those few words on unity, he then passed on after he brought his sons together.

# 32

### The Crafty Toad

A hunter used to go hunting together with his son. One day, they spotted an antelope that had hidden itself in the middle of a shrub and the hunters stealthily aimed at it and they speared the animal to death. They afterwards cut the antelope into two parts and then set off for their home but unfortunately, they lost their way in the thickest part of the woods.

The son complained: "Dad, we did not pass this way before; we did not come across these dense bushes!" Not even within a blink of an eye, a sound of a roaring lion was heard and it right away came into sight from the shady bushes and called out: "Little boy, can you swallow that antelope and then your father will swallow you and eventually I will swallow your father!" The father to the boy was very astonished and had mixed reactions as he prayed in his heart to God: "Help my son and I out of this incidence oh my God!"

Just from nowhere, a gigantic fire-belly toad joined them and interrupted the lion's orders. The enormous toad said: "That is true, you the young boy, can you please swallow the antelope and then your father will swallow you and the lion will swallow your father and after all, I will swallow the lion!"

Everyone stood still in fear and the toad yelled: "Please start swallowing yourselves quickly so that I can swallow too; I'm getting delayed!"

The lion was dumbfounded, and he said: "Hei folks, I will come back soon, wait for a minute." And the lion diplomatically disappeared into the hedges. Subsequently, the massive toad told the two hunters to leave immediately.

# 33

## A Fox and His Uncle, Kuony

Once upon a time in the land of animals' monarchy, there lived a fox and his uncle Kuony. They were neighbors and Kuony had only a red cow. One day, the fox thought about how he would have his uncle Kuony's red cow killed.

He left his home and went to his uncle Kuony's home and started calling him loudly when he got nearer his residence, he shouted: *"Thiaŋ is entering your cattle barn, luak! Thiaŋ is entering your cattle barn."*

His uncle Kuony heard him calling and he dashed out of his house without a delay while equipped with his sharp spears and a club and he blindly speared his cow to death in the heart.

Instantly, the fox came into the compound and pretended to be crying bitterly: "Why did you kill your cow yet I was telling you that the cow is entering into your *luak*? Take your *ahoth*, a bucket and fetch some water; I want you to bring plenty of water to be poured into the ears and mouth of this cow to recover her from this astound wound of the spear!"

Uncle Kuony and his wife speedily started their journey to the relatively far away river to bring some water. In no delay, the fox hurriedly skinned the cow and carried all the meat to his house. And when he saw his uncle and his wife coming from a distance, he promptly dug into the earth and inserted into it the cow's neck, leaving only the horns outside the ground. And he started to scream: *"Ye weŋ aciët jɔk!"* which is translated as: *the cow is being sunken by a Satan!*

His uncle came running and the fox asked him to come and assist him in pulling out the cow. As they were pulling the cow's head out of the ground, the fox was forcefully pushing it down rather and he complained that it should be pulled out gently to avoid chopping off the cow's head be-tween alor *jɔk and atueny wiën* (a location between the upper and lower part of a cow's neck). The two took a long time while pulling out the cow's head and in the long run, they finally pulled out the head, but the fox instantaneously blamed his uncle Kuony for not pulling out the cow's head gently.

He exclaimed: *"Yiec, kerkukuäu* (A fox's slogan for a surprise!) Didn't I tell you earlier that you need to pull out the cow's head with a great care?" He started to return to his homestead while singing his song.

His uncle uncovered the deception and earlier the next day, Kuony made up his mind on how he would trick the fox so that he should part-take in eating his cow's meat.

Earlier the following morning, Kuony transformed himself to be a beautiful girl who afterwards passed splendidly next to the fox's farmstead. He left what he was doing inside his *luak* after seeing the beautiful girl passing by and he went for her and approached her with both hands opened: "Hello my dear. Can I please know you by names, your clan and where you are residing?"

The two knew each other by names and they chatted for a quite long time before the fox could pass his love message to his new friend? And the strange girl quickly replied: "Okay. I have no problem in you marrying me if and only if you divorce your current wife!" Kuony replied: "There's no problem with that, it's not a big deal, and I'm going to split-up with her right now please!"

After a few words of courtship with the strange girl, the girl was convinced, and she was wel-comed into Mr. Fox's compound. Wonders shall never end; the fox hurriedly came and violently dismissed his wife! And the new wife remained free and started to handle her new household tasks with pleasure.

One day, the strange lady did not sit upright and the fox's children saw her below part and they exclaimed: "Hers resembles uncle Kuony's manhood!" And the fox immediately chased the chil-dren away as his partner cooked the cow's meat. And she delightfully consumed the meat as much as she wishes; moreover, she illegally carried some meat back to Kuony's residence. And at night when the fox asks for intimacy, she claimed to be on her period.

However, when the meat was over, the strange lady put it across that she was uncle Kuony but not a female anymore and changed herself in the presence of the fox! That left the fox speechless; and he was upset and unhappy for the mistake he had done by sending away his beloved wife! The fox went on a serious search for his wife and after he has found her, his wife refused to come back to a home where she was humiliated by being sent off. The fox remained single.

# 34

## The Puzzle of a Monster

I n an ancient time in the land of Chief Ajakchek, only one path led to a fishing camp, bur. One day, a horrible ogre appeared on that path and did not let people pass unless they answer a riddle, meek and he made an oath that he would die instantly if any person got the answer right!

The ogre, *Ajuɔŋ*, had a baboon's head and arms but a crocodile's tail. The riddle was this: "What creature moved on four feet in the morning, two feet in the afternoon, and three feet in the even-ing?" The wrong answer meant death.

Among the first few people to see *Ajuɔŋ* was the chief's son, Akuien. "Stand your ground and an-swer my riddle!" *Ajuɔŋ* shouted. "What creature moves on four feet in the morning, two feet in the afternoon, and three feet in the evening?" Akuien was a fearless gentleman but not that smart. "Is it a cow? A dog? I give up."

The next minute, *Ajuɔŋ* pounced on him and tore him apart.

The next day a young man named Wuol approached bur. "Stand your ground and answer my rid-dle! What creature moves on four feet in the morning, two feet in the afternoon, and three feet in the evening?" *Ajuɔŋ* shouted. Wuol was a very courageous person and smarter than Akuien.

"The creature must be man," he answered. "Man crawled on four legs in the morning of his life, walked on two in the afternoon, and in the evening of his life, he walked with the help of a stick."

Upon hearing the answer, *Ajuɔŋ*, flew into a rage and he died of a shock, when the tissues of his body did not receive adequate blood flow. From then onward, the residents of bur were freed from the terrorization by the ogre.

# 35

## An Eye For an Eye

A fox once set a deal in which all the hares' children were eaten up by a hungry dog. The hare made up his mind and found a way in which he could avenge the tragic loss of his beloved children. After making up his mind, he went to the cattle camp and found out that there was a dog which had just given birth and would rarely leave her puppies alone as they were too young to be left unattended.

After seeing where the dog lived, he returned to the forest and lied to the fox that there was a goat that had recently given birth to young ones but there was no one that took care of those puppies. The fox was very impressed and became curious about whether it was true or not.

"Are you sure that the young ones were really for a goat, but not for a dog?" the fox asked.

"Yes, I am sure, they are for a goat but not for a dog, as I know the differences between the young ones of a goat and a dog." the hare answered and he continued to explain further: "The dog has fluffy ears while the goat has erected ones, the latter has no claws while the previous has sharp ones and distinctively, the goat has got two teats while a dog has at most twelve teats and the dog's mouth has a long split towards its ears while the goat does not."

The fox was convinced and immediately requested the hare to take him to the site where he found the puppies. They took off to the cattle camp and after forty minutes, they reached the cattle camp and the hare led the fox up to the hut where the dog was, and he shouted: "You can now go alone and see by yourself the young ones of a goat inside the hut!"

The fox rushed into the hut and was surprised to see a different thing altogether! He found a hungry dog instead of the young ones of a goat! The fox tried his level best to make a U-turn but it was too late for him to escape.

He was caught in the process of dashing out of the hut and was impatiently eaten up by the starved dog within some few minutes. This was one of the rare incidences where the fox was outwitted by the hare. The hare felt happy after making the fox pay back for the awful death of her beloved children.

# 36

## The Ruined Relations

The man was a very great friend to two sister animals: the cow and the buffalo before they could break apart. There was no enmity at all between the three. They used to communicate in the same language and the dogs were their policemen. Whenever cows and buffaloes want to be milked, they could communicate it to the man and the man could get ready to milk his friends.

The man used to collect sufficient milk from all the cows and buffaloes. One afternoon, the man became stupid enough to spear a younger buffalo to death in the heart!

"What made you do that colleague?" the buffalo asked.

"Experience is gained through all these sorts of trials and practices!" the man grudgingly answered the question.

A terrible fight broke out instantly, but the cow did not bother to fight for the loss of her younger sister. On the contrary she assured her sister, the buffalo: "The man has ample spears and clubs; we will not manage revenge for our lost sister!"

"Shut up you coward!" The buffalo boomed at the cow. And the cow completely refused to fight the man and their talks ended up in disharmony.

The buffalo boldly fought the man alone and unluckily, she also lost her mother in the process. And on the other sides, the buffalo murdered four people. The buffalo declared it: "I will never ever stay with a man nor with my sister, the cow from today henceforth. And the man must pay back the price for the tragic loss of my beloved sister and a mother!"

The buffalo left the cow stranded and returned to the jungle for a continuous battle with man. The cow afterwards returned to her usual homestead to stay with the man although the man had slaughtered her dear sister and a mother.

# 37

*The Disgrace*

Two pairs of animals: the dog and the hyena on one side and the goat and the sheep on the other side travelled to a far village to date a beautiful girl. The first group of animals, the carnivores, were competing with the second group, the herbivores.

The first group that was composed of a dog and a hyena were the first to arrive at the lady's home and two hours later, the second group that was composed of a goat and a sheep arrived. Only one group of animals was supposed to sleep at the girl's compound to participate in a hot debate between them and the girl.

The other animals refused to leave by then as it was late at night and they remained standing in the compound until late night. As there were many mosquitoes around, the girl decided to accommodate the four animals in the same hut; two leather sheets were brought, one for the first group and the other one for the second group. And out of surprise, the herbivores chewed their cuds while the carnivores did not.

After a while, the dog thought that the herbivores were eating their leather sheet and he said to the hyena: "Hyena, please wake up and get out of this leather sheet; let us eat ours as well since our colleagues are eating theirs!"

The hyena straightaway woke up and found his opponents chewing their cuds and without a careful thought, he assumed that the guys were really consuming the leather sheet. "Yes, let us eat ours too," the hyena approved, and they entirely munched the leather sheet on which they were sleeping.

It was of a great surprise when the two teams' members woke up earlier the other morning; the second group's leather sheet was found while the dog and hyena were found lying on the ground and without a delay, they quit the site earlier to avoid being humiliated the following morning.

The first group members of carnivores left, and the second group of herbivores got the chance of enjoying some lengthy marriage conversations with the stunning girl.

# 38

## The Mistaken Identity

The cock was feared by all the animals and birds because of the red comb on his head; they thought it was a fire and they made him their leader. The animals used to provide him with grains, fruits and roots.

One day, a tiger and tigress returned to their homestead late in the evening and found out that their young ones were very hungry. The tigress rushed to the kitchen to prepare something for her children to eat but she found out that there was no fire! She sent her kids to fetch a fire from the cock's comb at the fowls' homestead.

The young ones went out and found the cock asleep; they were very confused of what to do; finally, they returned to their house and informed their parents that the cock had retired to his bed.

The tiger and tigress picked some tall dry grasses and instructed their young ones to bring the fire from the house where the cock was sleeping in. They moved slowly in line until they reached the house. The tiger stealthily entered and placed the dry grass onto the cock's comb, but it did not light at all! He placed them properly, but it did not light up the dry grasses.

He then touched the cock's comb, and it was just a cold skin. He immediately called in his wife and his kids to touch the comb as well!

They all touched it in turns, but it did not burn anyone, and they immediately yelled in chaos!

The cock immediately woke up and threated the tiger and his family members: "I will burn all of you right now!" The tiger responded by touching the cock's comb: "Yes, burn me right now fabricator!"

It was a great surprise and a discovery to the tiger and his family. The tiger said: "I'm going to inform all the birds and animals that you have been cheating and terrorizing the entire kingdom all along, yet your comb was not a fire!" The cock was almost to die of a shame before his wife and young ones but he finally made up his mind. The tiger and his family members rushed out of the poultry compound and they loudly called their neighbors to come and witness that the cock's comb was not a fire anymore!

The cock and all his relatives called for an urgent consultation and their discussion's outcome was to run away to a man's homestead for some help. They all left their compound to seek protection from the man. No sooner had the man warmly welcome the cock and his family members than they heard the rampaging voices of many neighboring animals and birds as they looted the poultry belongings inside their houses. That was when the man and poultry started to live together.

# 39

## The Disaster

A fly bit a snake's wound and the snake ran into a hole where a rat lived with her children. On seeing the snake entering the hole, the rat rang a bell to call his friend, the elephant to come to the rescue.

The elephant heard a ringing bell from the rat's homestead, and he expeditiously ran over to the rescue. On his way, the elephant accidentally stepped onto a turtle and in retaliation, the turtle released some toxic gas which immediately burnt up the whole forest and many lives of different species were eventually lost.

A vast woodlands and savanna lands got burnt up overnight and late the following afternoon, a thick smoke and soot condensed and formed acid rain which rained in all the regions. It flooded the areas and corroded the roofs of many buildings and scorched the vegetation.

Different species of animals and plants were submerged and farmers were displaced. At last, many animals said, "An accident by an individual can jeopardize the lives of many other different spices."

# 40

## The Domestic Mystery

After a husband and a wife had produced their two kids, their relationship went sour. The lady became querulous and disobedient until she was divorced. After she had gained her senses at her parents' home, she tried extremely hard to convince her husband to allow her to come back to stay with her kids but it was too late for the husband to admit her back!

She resorted to visiting a witchdoctor instead. She narrated the whole of the story to the magician and her point was to go back to her home to stay together with her kids. The witchdoctor promised her that she would eventually be reunited with her husband if she accomplished the task that she would be assigned to undertake.

The witchdoctor sent her to go and fetch a lion's whisker from his mustaches and bring it back to him after she had found one. She agreed and went into the forest looking for a lion while pulling a goat. After six days of a serious search, she found a lion and daringly approached the beast. On reaching near it, she released the goat to the beast. The lion afterwards got hold of the goat and hungrily consumed it. Afterwards, the lady returned home and returned to the same site the following morning carrying another goat and she handed over the goat to the lion.

On the third day, she came with a third goat and handed the goat to the lion. On seeing the goat, the lion was pleased with the lady as he swung his tail. The lady handed over the goat to the lion as she held it by a rope. Since the lion trusted the lady, he did not bother to doubt the lady even if she could come closer to him and touch him by his cheeks and ears as well and he did not react.

The lady pulled out a whisker in the process of grooming the beast. And left him eating his goat and she proceeded to the witchdoctor's compound and gave him the whisker. "My dear friend, how did you remove a whisker from a lion?" the witchdoctor asked.

"It took me three days to befriend the lion," she explained. "I had to provide him with a goat for three consecutive days and on the third day, I came nearer and slowly approached him and removed it." The lady happily narrated the story as she waited for her promised solution.

The witchdoctor said: "If you could manage to befriend a wild animal, how could you not befriend your own husband? Join your husband right now and mind you, you need to befriend him the same way you befriended the lion and you will be welcome back my dear." And the lady immediately got a chance of being welcomed back home.

# 41

## Akeerpiou and the Monster

Once upon a time, there lived many pastoralists who set-tled across the swampy area, *toic,* where they used to graze their cattle. There were many lions and monsters. One day, during their transhuman period, the ladies were walking in a group and they remained behind along the River Nile's tributaries.

From a nearby bush, a monster transformed itself into a human be-ing and joined the young ladies who were just relaxing after they had quenched their thirst as the cattle were near. He slowly approached them and immediately asked: "I am thirsty; can you please provide me with some water?" One of the ladies immediately stood up to fetch some water for the stranger and she replied: "Surely, I will provide you with some water."

Unexpectedly, the stranger poured away the water that was given to him by the young girl and he yelled again: "Can you once again give me some water please?" He was handed the water but he refused to pick up the calabash of water from the girl.

"Why are you refusing to receive the calabash of water yet you asked for some water?" The young girl angrily asked the stranger.

"I wish this calabash of drinking water would be handed over to me by that young lady," he gave his opinion as he pointed to a young and a most beautiful one named Akeerpiou in the middle of the other girls.

Akeerpiou agreed and moved forward, and she received the calabash of water from her colleague and handed it over to the peculiar man. Just within a wink of an eye in the process of handing the water over to him, the outlandish man deliberately dropped the calabash of drinking water and he firmly grabbed and pulled Akeerpiou into the sudd swamp which was jam-packed with reeds and papyrus. And the other girls ran away.

The strange man gradually changed himself to be a monster moderately and when Akeerpiou saw him transforming, she unswervingly wrestled with him at her full strength. And at last, she managed to escape from the grasper. She ran away speedily, and the monster tried his level best to catch her, but he missed her by inches. Akeerpiu ran as fast as her thin skeleton legs could carry her to where she would find someone to give her a hand.

Akeerpiou did not give up as she was fit to run for a long time. She did not give up after a long chase until they reached the village of a chief, Tong who had many young and brave youngsters. The lady enthusiastically continued to run until she approached a large group of conversing young men in an open field.

The lady reached the young men and when she wanted to halt, she did not control herself and she fell onto a ground with a heavy thud. The bouncy gentlemen who were properly equipped up to their teeth rushed towards the beast. As many people put it: 'many hands make work lighter,' and the beast died within a very short time after many spears landed on him.

The gentlemen returned to the lady after they have killed the monster and whenever they asked her, she could not manage to talk. Thus, they sent their younger brother to go and come with their father to the site to witness the incident by himself. Their father arrived and luckily, the lady recovered her lost mind and she started to respond positively to some few questions that were being asked. The old man ordered his daughters to take her home and he said: "Feel at home my daughter, you are safe and in the right hands so far."

After she had rested, she managed to narrate the whole story to the girls; and later, to the host, Chief Tong. The old man then knew her clan as 'a responsible and courageous one.' Akeerpiou spent a couple of days before she was provided with young men, Ajak, Nai-Nai and Tongthi to take her up to her home. Back at home, Akeerpiou was reported to have been eaten up by the monster by the girls who were then dispersed by the beast.

They spent a day on the way and on the second day, they reached her home at midnight when everyone had slept. Akeerpiou called her mother to open the door but she refused to open it and said: "My ancestors, how can my dead daughter hail me? What wrong have I done? Leave me alone please!" Others in the hut were also confused and they remained dumb founded.

She moved to her stepmother and repeated the same: "Please my stepmother, open the door for me, this is me, Akeerpiou." "Are you serious? If your own mother could refuse to let you in, who am I to recognize your voice? Go away and let us sleep in peace please!"

She returned to the doorstep of her mother and said: "Mama, can't you recognize my voice? Why do you deny me access to enter our house? Did I have any problem with you when I left for the cattle camp?"

Her mother was almost convinced, and she asked: "Who are those people walking with you?" Her mother asked.

"They are children of Chief Tong Tong and they are Nai-Nai, Tongthi and Ajak," Akeerpiou replied. "No! No! Not at all, get away; I do not know those people with those names!"

She sat down outside her mother's hut as she sang a song of disappointment: "My own people are denying me entry, what can I do? My own mother is denying me entry, what can I do? My own father and siblings are keeping quiet, what can I do?"

After she has completed singing her own song, she returned to the doorstep of her mother's house and repeated pleading: "My dear mother, please just open the door and check on me." And her mother replied, "Go away, my daughter Akeerpiou is dead!" Luckily, her father cocked his voice and said: "Open the door and let us check on her." The young ones in the room were in a celebratory mood as they chuckled and stood still.

The door was opened and out of a surprise, it was found out that it was a real Akeerpiou not a ghost. Her own mother cried out loudly and pleaded for forgiveness from her daughter who afterwards said: "No reason for you to cry mum, let us all praise God that I am alive."

What a celebration there was that night and the following days! They shared in joy by slaughtering two big bulls. People gathered and they conducted thanksgiving prayers for their lost and found daughter, Akeerpiou.

Akeerpiou re-counted the unabridged story, and the children of Chief Tong were appreciated for their good work, and afterwards, they were told to greet their father. And after the prayers, they returned to their home village.

After some months, one of the children to Chief Tong, Ajak, was in love and wanted to marry Akeerpiou and thus, he approached his father and broke the ice. His father gave him permission as he was aware of her family lineage. Ajak with his brothers returned to Akeerpiou's homestead and the young men informed Akeerpiou and her sisters about their interest in marrying her. And she had no objections as she knew the young man.

She then after transferred the young men to her elder sisters and the elder sisters afterwards referred the case to their young mothers who finally informed their elderly mothers. After that chain of communication, the elderly mothers passed the message to the father and the uncles of the girl who afterwards informed his kinsmen. Subsequently, the marriage procedures were followed until the two clans met and negotiated on the bride price in good faith. After the payment of the bride price, marriage seals were made when each party slaughtered some bulls as an exchange their gifts. At last, Akeerpiou's marriage was a blessed one and they were happily married as husband and wife.

# 42

### The Drunken Guinea Fowls

The villagers used to till their farms in unison to encourage each other on the effectiveness and efficiency of teamwork before the rains could start. They prepared a local brew to motivate and boost their morale and energy as they worked. After they were done with their work, they took more of the local stuff and rested for a while as they took a nap.

One day when the farmers were taking a nap, the brothers to hens, the guinea fowls, saw the calabashes of local brew and they rushed towards them as they thought they may contain some water. They rushed into the shade and collectively quenched their thirst by drinking from the calabashes of alcohol. One farmer woke up just after some few minutes and found the guinea fowls all drunk. The birds staggered around as they tried to gain their balance to move away but they didn't.

That farmer who witnessed the incident woke up the rest of the farmers and after they confirmed it, they all praised God for the gift of guinea fowls. They picked up their hoe handles and subsequently hit the guinea fowls on their heads and necks. And after a while, they stopped each other from killing plenty of them and advised that they should get hold of a few of them alive as they would be good farm birds. This was how the man came to rear the guinea fowls on his farms.

# 43

## The Narrow Escape

Most elderly people who could not sometimes manage to migrate with the people from place to place would burden their most energetic ones at times of relocation. Many cattle keepers used to migrate from one place to another as they look for greener pastures. One day, the relatives met for a long time to discuss their migration plans.

It came out from their meeting that the two most elderly grand-mothers and a young lady should be left enclosed in a cattle barn. They were provided with whatever food they would require during a dry season. Their three granaries were all filled up with balanite tree nuts, heer, sorghum and mil-let; they were also provided with both dry meat and fish. And the old women were enclosed into the cattle barn with enough water in many big pots for that season.

The old women had to cook inside their cattle barn and they would not go outside as they fear at-tacks from the wild animals. However, the youngest lady among the women repetitively sang: *"Chuai luak; aba ciet adan ee pil; aba ciet angui-ku-dhuony; cin ne koor cam yow!"* which is literally translated as: *'I gained weigh within a cattle barn; until I appear round like a traditional grinding stone; until I look like hyena-baobab (bouncy); I wish the lion could eat me up lol!'*

After two months, they were bored of staying indoors! "Is it pos-sible for us to get out of this cattle barn at least to get a fresh air outside and to have a shower at nearby water pool?" The young lady suggested: "Yes, it's possible." They all moved out of the cattle barn for a shower and a fresh air.

A lion quickly snuck into the cattle barn while the three inhab-itants were still outside. And after they were done, they returned to their cattle barn. At night, the lion roared and one of them said: *kɔ̈r acë hët në abär män Ajak,* which is translated as: *the lion is quite far as it roars at the balanite tree of the mother to Ajak.* Just within a short time, it roared again within the cattle barn and the other lady said: *kɔ̈r acië hët në aguene män Kɔ̈ɔ̈c,* which is translated as: *the lion has finally come closer to us as it roars at the balanite tree of the mother to Koch.* And at last, it roared at an impressive voice and the three collectively yielded: *"It's roaring inside here at our cattle barn!"*

They lit the fire and surely, they found out that the lion was inside with them and the lion said: "You the three residents must go for a wrestling competition and whoever wins will not be eaten up by me!" The young lady defeated the two elderly women and she thought she would be par-doned. Ironically, the lion ate her straight away.

As the lion was busy consuming the young lady, one of the elderly women drew the lion's atten-tion by shouting out loudly: "Alash! The youth are returning; I tell you; they are all returning from the cattle camp!"

"Where will I run to for my own security?" The lion enquired. "Get out through where you entered and hide yourself in the very shallow well besides the balanite tree, *thäu,*" one of the elderly wom-en suggested.

The lion quickly found his way out of the cattle barn and ran into the deepest well and he at that point broke his neck straightaway. The elderly women heard the thundering echo of the dropping lion into the deepest well and they celebrated: "Hurrah! How lucky are we! The lion has really made it into the deepest well, how lucky are we!" Finally, the two elderly women immediately closed the opening where the lion exited and they stayed inside the cattle barn until their children and grandchildren returned from the cattle camp at the swamplands, *toic*.

# 44

---◦◯◦---

## *The Borrowed Tail*

L ong, long ago in the jungle of *Cuɔl-Akɔl*, all the animals used
to come together at the end of the year to parttake in their
annual sport festivals. They stayed peacefully and whenever
there were is–sues, they ironed them out amicably before their king,
his majesty, the lion.

By the end of the fiscal year, they competed once again through a
dancing stiff competition and whoever emerged a winner was to be
given a very weighty award. And the award was whatever the winner
asked for.

The next morning before the dancing competition could start; the
sheep hurriedly went to the dog's dynasty and seriously asked to bor-
row his tail as she was aiming to emerge as the winner for that year.
The dog refused but the sheep earnestly begged the dog until the dog
agreed to give it to her for that competition period only.

Afterwards, the dancing competition kicked off and all the animals
performed, and by the end of the competition, adjudicators ranked
the participants' marks. And the final list for the dancers was given to
the chief guest for the announcement starting from the unfortunate
performers to the out–standing ones.

The sheep did not hear her name and all the other animals' names were called out and, in the end, the chief guest said: "This fiscal year award goes to none other than the sheep!" There was a great uproar as the animals cherished the great achievement of their partner. And subsequently the sheep was called forward and asked: "Congratulations fellow sheep; what gift would you demand from us to be given to you?" The elephant asked. "Fix the tail that I'm wearing to be mine forever!" The sheep demanded.

"Yes, your request is heard," the elephant acknowledged it and he continued to ask the entire ani-mals' kingdom members: "Can we fix the tail that the sheep has right now to be his forever?" The elephant enquired. "Yes, make it possible right away. Make it possible in her favor right now." All the animals seconded it, except the dog, the owner of the tail!

The animals' collective decision was final and the dog's tail was fixed on the sheep's body. And the sheep's tail remained with the dog. However, it was too late for the dog to complain about her tail.

The dog resorted to fierce fighting with the sheep and the sheep hastily ran away up to the man's homestead where she was rescued from being eaten up by the angry dog. Afterwards, the sheep congratulated the man for protecting him. And in return, the sheep gave her milk and meat to man for the protection. Whenever a sheep sees a dog passing by, he says: "An anus is passing over there in search of his tail for covering itself!"

# 45

## A Life For Life

Aman was peacefully playing with his children when the hawks speedily appeared chasing a dove. And the dove penetrated the leaves of the tree and then descended and perched on the man's head. The man was very astonished, but he did not scare it off. Luckily, the hawks went on their way and the dove caught the children's attention.

"This is my bird, it's my bird, bring it for me; it's my bird, give it to me baba," all the children struggled to get hold of the dove but their dad refused to give it to anyone among his children. He quickly concealed the dove in his overall and lied to his children: "The dove has just flown away!" The children agreed and they continued to play with their father. After their play, their father in-structed them to return to their mother and their father afterwards released the dove secretly and it flew away safely.

After a day, the dove returned and perched on the very tree where the man used to play with his children. The dove found him playing with his kids and it started to communicate in their local lan-guage: *"Pïïr ee pïïr, jälke. Pïïr ee pïïr, jälke, wäkɔnnë, abënnë raan de ater kɔc yɔ̈tyic, jälke!"* Which is translated as: *Life is for life, leave, life is life, leave; tonight, the enemy will attack you, leave!*

At that very time, he informed his family members and the neighbors about what he had heard from the dove but people did not believe what he was saying; they mocked him instead. The man returned to his home and instructed his wife to get ready for the journey. They then left the village with his family members altogether with their animals that day and the enemy attacked their village that night. Many lives were lost, and all the cattle raided, and assets were looted.

# 46

## *The Tiger's Skin*

Numerous paramount chiefdoms have special considerations for those powerful chiefs and magi-cians who wear tigers' hides. It's perceived as a symbol of power and dignity for one's eminence related to brevity and intelligence. It also acts as an emblem of supremacy amongst others. An inci-dent happened at one of the rural villages where chiefs used to go to their small nearby town to set-tle their subjects' disputes and later return to their homes in the evening. There was one of the chiefs who used to wear an interesting tiger's skin which cost him five heads of cattle to barter. The tiger's skin was a very wide and colourful one.

The chief was to lose his tiger's skin when it was almost stolen by unknown gunmen in the even-ing when he was returning home from the town. He was ambushed in the forest when he was near his house; unknown armed men stopped him, and they shouted: "Are you a man or a tiger?" And the chief replied: "I'm a man." And they continued to ask more questions: "If you are a man, can you please come out of the tiger's skin and move backward without looking for-ward? And if you are a tiger, can you jump up the tree?" And the chief replied: "Yes, I will come out of the tiger's skin."

Instantly as the chief was trying to remove the exciting tiger's skin before he placed it down and moved backward, many armed youths who attended their marriage ceremony in one of the nearby villages suddenly reached the scene where the chief was undressing himself!

And they immediately asked: "*Bäny*, boss, why are you undressing yourself on the way?" And the chief replied: "Because the way wants me to do it so!" He answered the question as he points to-wards the direction where the robbers were. No sooner did the robbers saw the many youths com-ing towards them than they rushed into the forest and were nowhere to be seen.

Fortunately, the young men exclusively comprehended the whole story, and they swiftly ran after them in the said direction. Luckily, just within some few minutes, they got hold of all the culprits and they were beaten up and maimed badly as they were being led to their small town for jailing. In the end, the robbers did not get away with the chief's vibrant tiger skin and they regretted a lot as they waited for their trials at the correctional center.

# 47

═══◦◉◦═══

## *The Black Crows*

Once upon a time, there lived a stubborn young man who was fond of catching and piercing the black crows' eyes. There were many crows in his village and he designed traps for catching them. He was used to catching them, pierce their eyes and absurdly enjoyd watching them as the birds helplessly dart and flap around in miserable conditions before he could leave them.

He had been doing this nasty act since his childhood. However, he resorted to fighting his age mates whenever they warned him not to participate in such a cruel act and he totally switched off his mind from absorbing any of their pieces of advice.

After a long time, the gentleman got married and consequently, his first-born baby girl was born blind. And to make things worse, his wife gave birth to a second child and he was also born blind. In so doing, he came to his senses and approached his father and narrated everything to him; what he used to do earlier in his childhood times when he was fond of piecing birds' eyes.

His father requested his relatives and friends to come to his house-hold to hear by themselves what his son has revealed before they could pray to *Nhialic*, God via their ancestors to forgive the young boy for his unfeeling acts. Their concern was to ask *Nhialic* earnestly to free and clean their son from the cases and bad omens brought by his bad deeds. When their prayers and chants were over, all the people ate and drank adequately before they returned to their homes. Fortunately, after a year, the young man's wife was blessed with a third child; a baby boy whose sight was okay.

# 48

## *The Crushed Rapport*

The hawk and the cock were great friends; they stayed together in one compound. The two and their children co-existed for a very long time before their permanent conflict began.

One evening, the hawk did not cook after he realized that they had run out of salt and the cock promised that he would go to their nearby town the following morning to buy some salt and other goods if the weather was promising. The cock then started his journey earlier the following morning before the rest could wake up. He went to the town and bought all the items he prioritized to buy.

As he started his journey back home, the load he carried was quite weightier and he had to rest for a while in a shade near their home. The hawk came and got surprised when he found a cock standing on one leg as he had hidden the other leg beneath his wings.

The hawk asked: "Why you are on one leg sir; where is your other leg?" The cock responded: "I have exchanged it with a salt!" And the hawk continued to ask: "If I go to the town right now, will I also be able to get the shopkeeper that exchanges a leg for some salt?" And the cock replied: "Surely, you will get him, but you need to hurry up before the salt finishes."

The hawk swiftly rushed to the town and asked the shopkeeper: "I want to exchange my one leg with a salt!" The shopkeeper stared at him and he found it out that the hawk really meant his statements and the shopkeeper replied: "Come in here please and hand me your thigh." The hawk entered the shop and handed over his thigh and it was surely chopped off instantly and he was given two kilograms of salt.

It really gave him an awfully hard time to carry the load home as he limped and bled amply. However, he was very amazed after reaching their home when he saw the cock on his two legs again: "How come you are on your two legs again; yet you exchanged your one leg with a salt?"

And the cock replied: "No, I did not exchange my leg with a salt; you must be a very stupid fellow; I just lied to you because you bothered me a lot with your silly questions!" The cock and his young ones mockingly laughed at the hawk as he regretted desperately for the poor decision he has made.

The hawk was very annoyed and furious; however, he did not manage to attack the cock as the ailing wound at his thigh prevented him from attacking the cock and his chicks immediately. That was the very genesis of the hatred between the hawk and the cock. Whenever a hawk sees a chick wandering around, he promptly grabs it and hovers away with it in revenge.

# 49

## The Bleeding Hyena

Long, long ago in one of the African rainforests, there lived a
hyena and his nephew, the hare. They were hunters and gatherers. They also used to go deep into the forest to collect honey. The hare was good at collecting fruits and roots while the hyena
was the best at hunting small animals.

One day, the hare brought home honey and made the hyena hav a
taste as well. "Wow! What a sweet substance! Where did you collect it
from?" The hyena asked the hare. "I collected it in the woods; would
you like to come with me for its harvest tomorrow?" The hare asked.
They agreed that they would go for its collection the following day.

Earlier, the following morning, they set off for the honey collection. And after a while, they reached the site where the honey was
positioned, and the hare advised: "Honey is collected while an idle
animal is tied to a tree to avoid unnecessary movements." And absent-
mindedly, the hyena agreed.

The hyena was tied down to the tree while the hare harvested the
honey, shockingly he left with all the honey and left the hyena tangled
to the tree. Afterwards, the swarm of bees angrily attacked the hyena.
He was stung severally all over his body until he became unconscious.

Coincidentally, he broke the ropes which he was tied onto the tree and fled into the savanna grassland with vigor.

Later, he tremblingly moved his own way until he reached home lately in the evening. Immediately when he reached the compound, the hyena sniffed some roasted fish and he shouted: "did I really smell something right? Is it true that you have prepared some fish for us to eat?" Over there at home, the hare had roasted five big mudfish, *Protopterus aethiopicus* and he kept them outside the hyena's house so as to induce the materialistic animal.

The hyena at that very moment forgot to ask why the hare tied him to the tree but he hungrily proceeded to eat his roasted fish. He afterwards inquisitively asked where he got the fish from as he was not fully satisfied: "Where did you get this nice mudfish from my dear?" And the hare answered: "I fished these mudfish right there at the swamps, would you mind coming with me tomorrow for another fishing expedition?" And the hyena answered: "Yes, I will come with you tomorrow morning for the fishing expedition."

They got prepared for the harpooning voyage the following morning and they walked for three hours before they reached the mudfish pond, which was covered with water lilly, *goor* and water hyacinth; *Eichhornia Crassipes*, 'Marum-toic'. The hare afterwards cleared off *goor* and *marum-toic* and ordered the hyena to draw the mudfish out of the fishpond with his external organ. The naïve animal agreed to do it so as he was told! However, he did not think twice either to lower it into the pond straightaway or not!

Unfortunately, a big mudfish instantly got hold of the hyena's manhood and antagonistically bit it off and the beast cried out loudly in anguish: "Oops! Oops! It has chopped off my lower part!"

Unfeelingly, the hare ended up laughing out loudly and he warned his colleague: "Once beaten, twice shy!" Subsequently, the mudfish returned into its hiding place after he had swallowed the stuff; that was when the mudfish developed the long black cord (*cuol*) inside its stomach! In the end, the hyena bled profusely as he hurriedly run into the forest regretting: "I wish I knew not to trust the hare's instructions previously!"

# 50

## The Wildly Living

Over centuries, many African tribes divide their generations into age sets and age groups. Many age groups form an age set. Wars were fought as per either age sets or age groups depending on the magnitude of the fighting.

Over time, much age setting deterioration has been brought about by modernity and that initiated mixed social contact between the senior and the junior age groupings. Urbanization took roots in age groups' hearts in some communities and many of the men adopted civilization. The most elderly people have called for their cultural custody and heritage, but it was all miscarried in the youngsters' hearts! The school going young men were warned against theft, drunkenness, idleness and the attending of night clubs in towns while the communities guarding ones were advised to be more watchful and bold like their ancestors who protected their territories and dignity.

However, they did not get the elderly advice right; they took it as bad motives altogether which prevented them from exploiting their youth-hood opportunities. One day, the youth rebelled against the aged and went deeply into the forest where they extensively discussed how they would get rid of their distressing elderly men. Eventually, all the young men finally concluded that they would kill all their fathers and grandfathers who happened to be in the age groups and age sets ahead of theirs as this would pave them a way to decide and perform whatever decision they wish to accomplish.

They unanimously agreed that each one of their group would kill his father and grandfather if they were both alive. But among them, their most courageous and wise man named Deng disputed the idea, however, the notion of the majority took the lead. Deng did not agree with what they were advocating for and they tried to coax him which was futile.

Deng then exited from the group and he was identified by some of his colleagues as an obstacle to their developmental agendas and plans, in so doing, they concluded that they would kill their parents. Unfortunately, all the other young men killed their parents and grandparents, but Deng's father and grandfather were not killed. And they raided many bulls as they went deeply into the forest for leisure after they had achieved their goals.

They slaughtered their healthier bulls and joyfully celebrated over there in the woods as the rest of their mothers were busy burying their dead husbands and fathers back at home. After a week, their age mate, Deng joined them again however, he found one of his colleagues in a miserable condition.

A snake that was chasing a frog mistakenly entered his friend's mouth and moved through his aesophagus until its head appeared at end of the victim's rectum. The leader of the defiance team monologued: "If we could get a wise man that could separate this young man from the snake, we will really appreciate the opportunity."

Deng replied: "And if I bring an elder, will you people not kill him?" Their leader replied: "No! Not exactly my brother, we will not kill him but will appreciate him relatively for the great work he has done among us by helping one of our resilient team members."

Deng agreed: "Okay, I will swiftly go and tirelessly search for an elder who can help you out of this problem." Deng went home and informed his father about the incident and they quickly rushed to

the site where the young men were all astonished. The chairperson to
the gang explained how it happened up to the very point the snake
entered the young man through his gullet.

The wise elder instructed all the young men to go and search for
a frog after he had keenly listened to the entire story. Within some
few minutes, a frog was caught and brought straightaway and he tied
a string around the frog's leg. He then pulled the frog next to the rear
end where the snake's head was appearing.

The snake saw the frog and whenever it stretched its neck to
catch it, the old man pulled the string. He repetitively brought and
pulled the frog to and fro the young man's body until the snake finally
stretched its muscles and completely dragged itself out of the rectum.

Luckily, the young man was finally set free. Deng and his father
were appreciated by the foulmouthed team members for their wise
decisions. And the wise were right to say: "What can be seen by an old
man while seated cannot be seen by a child while standing."

# 51

## The Pangs of Hatred

O ne day, a humble wife to a policemen who hated dogs naturally was ill-fated when her husband brought home a one-month-old puppy despite her not being consulted. The puppy was well cared for; he was used to eating good and healthier foods and was fed thrice a day with plenty of milk, which made him grow up very fat.

The puppy became very healthier as he was well-fed and groomed. And the young dog became knowledgeable and vigilant on security-related-matters since his master used to take him regularly for training at the nearby police dogs station. Then the dog started his own duties of guarding his master's compound and he started hunting wild game within a period of just five months.

Unfortunately, his master passed on one night, and things turned out from bad to worse. The wife did not properly look after the young dog that was used to frequent dog food and milk. But only the elder sons to the deceased could irregularly provide him with a little food. The wife neglected the dog upto the point of starvation.

The dog was much starved. One morning, the dog salivated when he saw the wife to his master passing next to his kennel carrying meat as she returned from butchery. The wife saw the dog salivating and violently shouted while pointing a dog with a knife: "Even if you dribble saliva as much as a liter, I will not provide you even with a naked bone, period!"

The meat was cooked, and all the family members ate until they were much satisfied. And to make things worse, the wife to the late collected all the leftovers plus the cleared bones and marched outside her house and unfeelingly threw all the remnants into a pit latrine. The dog was disgusted as he shouted in the lady's native language: "Why are you that cruel and unfair to me madam? What is all this enmity about?"

The lady did not have any time to apprehend this very incidence where the dog could manage to talk in her own language! She dashed into the kitchen and returned carrying an axe and immediately started to demolish the dog's kennel. The deceased's eldest son intervened and untied the dog from his chain after he has realized that his own mother was planning to kill the innocent dog!

The dog was freed, and he ran into the neighborhood. Things turned out to be better over there as the dog could move from one compound to another searching for something to eat. He also teamed up with other dogs and had fun and that made him more accompanied. In the end, he recalled how nice his master was and planned to return home.

He then returned home, and no news was good news. In conclusion, the wife to the deceased did not allow the dog once again to enter her own compound despite her children's supplication. And the dog disappeared once more into the town. However, the harsh lady did not think twice about the security concerns of her compound.

One night, a gang of thieves broke into her compound a couple of weeks after the dog left. They entered and intimidated everyone in the compound to surrender whatever valuable goods and items they had. And in the end, they carried away all the valuable items they found. Earlier in the following morning, all her neighbors were astonished how the thieves managed to enter the compound when the compound had a police-trained dog. And the cruel lady regrettably cried out: "I wish I knew not to chase away my husband's dog, to alert me when the strangers were breaking into my compound!"

# 52

## *The Revenge*

I n the ancient animals' society, there lived great friends: a giraffe and its young one and a fox. They were living peacefully together in an abandoned old building, opposite to the river where the man lived along its banks. Many farmers had their big plantations at the other side of the river where they grew a variety of cereals, fruits and vegetables. One day, the fox approached the giraffe and his young one and informed them about the ripe fruits at the other side of the river and the giraffes' appetite of eating some fruits made her to accept the invitation.

They set off to look for fruits earlier the next morning, and over at the bank, the giraffe and its young one decided to offer the fox a ride, and he was carried on the back of the giraffe as they crossed a two-meter-deep river. Then they quickly rushed into the garden where they started to eat the man's fruits.

After a while, the fox was satisfied and his crafty outlook incited him to shout: "Hey the giraffes, I want to sing my favorite song?" And the giraffes immediately complained: "No! No please, not now, we are not yet satisfied, you will sing your own song when we are all done." He again ar-gued: "It's my right time to sing; whom shall I wait for?"

He busted into his own songs: *"Yiɛc! kërkukuäu. Xɛn rɛɛc akiirkië të cän ke dɔt ci mën de abuɔi,"* which is translated as: *Alas! My plans are terrible after I had interwoven them like a net!*

The owner of the garden heard the fox singing and urgently picked up a stick and immediately came to the site where he found the giraffe and her young one trying to escape. But the fox was nowhere to be seen. He speedily ran away and halted at the riverbank where he waited for his friends whom he left behind to come and offer him a ride!

The owner of the garden badly beat up the giraffe's young one to death and its mother in the end managed to escape with major injuries all over her body. She afterwards rested besides the riverbank before she could strain to walk to the site where the fox ran to.

The fox saw the giraffe approaching and rushed to welcome her as his crocodile tears roll down his face. "Where is your younger one?" The fox asked. "The man has murdered her," the giraffe an-swered. And the giraffe ridiculously comforted the pretending fox by saying: "Cry not my friend but thank God that you and I are all safe; shut up please and let us cross the river earlier before it gets dark." They moved to the crossing point and the giraffe instructed his friend to climb onto her back as they cross the river.

They went on their way while quiet and after they have reached the middle of the river, the giraffe shouted: "I want to take a shower over here please! I always dive my body whenever I have come to a deeper side of the river." And the fox disputed her statement: "No, please, take me first to the other side of the river and then you can return to take a shower later!"

All his arguments did not make any sense to the giraffe and she abruptly knelt to submerge all her body, besides only a quarter of her neck remained above the water. The fox was carried away by the water current and the giraffe moved out of the river after she saw that the fox being carried away by the current. And finally, the giraffe whispered: "Tit for tat sometimes heals a broken heart."

# 53

## The Animals' Severance

Back in the day, the giant animals were all feared and the elephants were the most feared ones among the mighty ones. All the animals were used to looking after cattle; they were all used to herding their cattle. During summer, they migrated to *toic* and by spring, they returned home. Animals migrated from place to place as seasons changed. Whenever the animals arrived at their destination, the elephant put up with his cattle in the middle of the cattle camp. At a time when there were cases of cattle rustlers, the elephant's cows were not raided as they were in the middle of the cattle camp. And the smallest animals like mongoose, *agoor* settled at the periphery of the cattle camp where raiders frequently stole cattle from.

Earlier in the beginning of autumn, the animals migrated to new locations where there were green pastures for their cows at the banks of River Nile.

The hare came and ordered *agoor* to settle in the middle of cattle camp where the elephants' cattle were kept after a serious lobby. And *Agoor* confidently agreed and placed his cattle pegs in the middle of the cattle camp where the elephant used to put up his!

The elephant was surprised when he came to realize that *agoor* had settled in the middle of the cattle camp where he used to put up with his cattle. The elephant aggressively approached *agoor's* location and violently pulled out *agoor's* cattle pegs one by one and sadistically threw them away. *Agoor* reacted aggressively by throwing a peg at the elephant's cheeks; and the peg's sharp end pierced and broke into the beast's upper jaw muscles.

The elephant was disappointed and wanted to grind *agoor* into fragments, but he did not manage to get hold of him. *Agoor's* relatives ran away out of the cattle camp. And after some minutes, the hare passed by pretending that he had not either seen or heard any sort of the violence between the two animals and he exclaimed: "Hei! Colleague, what has happened with your cheeks?"

"It's *agoor* that threw a sharp peg into my cheeks," the elephant responded. "I will help you out of this problem by removing the piece of wood from your cheeks," the hare suggested.

Late in the evening the hare came to the elephant section carrying his tools for operating the elephant's cheek. The hare's dramatic irony was later uncovered by the elephant after his lips were dismantled through the hare's bogus operation where his checks were transformed!

The hare cut off chunks of meat at the giant's lips and cheeks and threw them into a pot of boiling water. And he claimed that if the masses of meat were not cut off around his cheeks and lips, the elephant would develop *liir,* tuberculosis of the glands. The hare as a doctor mixed hot and cool water to obtain a lukewarm one for cleaning the beast's wounds. At last, the hare located and removed a piece of peg that remained in the elephant's cheek; he removed it and showed it to the elephant. And the elephant had a keen look at the piece of peg and was upset for what a tiny animal has done to him and he unhappily left.

Afterwards, the hare invited all his friends, man included to have a dinner with him. They all gathered, and they were surprised after tasting the cooked chunks of elephant's meat:

"Waw! What a delicious meat! Which animal's meat is it?" The man asked. "It's an elephant's meat; I cut it off when I was operating him," the hare answered. The invited team quickly ate the meat but they were not satisfied. And they still longed for more meat of the kind, earlier the following morning.

They eventually decided and teamed up to fight the elephants for their delicious meat. They killed many elephants and a few escaped into the forest. Animal to animal fighting then after broke out and that was the very day man started to hunt for the elephants. Other animals like hyena started to eat the sheep and the goats while the lions jumped onto the cows. The animals' camp was in uproar; it turned out to be a carnivores eating herbivores camp and all were on the run.

The hare came and whispered to a man; "Go and mark the water point as yours right away as the animals eat themselves, some have run out of the cattle camp." The lion took all the cows; hyena took all the goats and sheep.

Weaver bird, *amour* took control of all the grains. And when the carnivores were satisfied and felt very thirsty, they all ran to the water point where they found a man guarding the water source!

The lion was the first to arrive at the water point and he quarreled with the man on who owned the water source. And the man prevented the lion from having a drink unless the lion handed over his cattle to him. However, the lion gave in by giving his cattle to the man in exchange for drinking water. The hyena afterwards arrived with his goats and sheep and was also refused to drink some water. He later gave in and handed over his goats and sheep to the man after a prolonged argument. Many more animals came in turns and their possessions were collected by the man in exchange for drinking water.

The last to come was the weaver bird who also handed over its grains after two days' negotiations period with the man after it finally realized that there was no way out.

The man eventually acquired all the cattle, sheep, goats and the grains and there afterwards left to clear a less thick forest besides a water source where he built his own residence. That was how the man attained all his wealth.

# 54

---

## The Battle of Wit

A sheep went far into the jungle to eat lots of secondary growth of grass (*Nyuɔ̈p*) after the savanna grassland vegetation was burnt. The lion and his cousin, the hyena, also went to that vicinity for a hunt. The two carnivals spotted an antelope which they afterwards attacked and consumed within a short time.

The two animals again spotted a sheep which they just captured within some few minutes. They seized and interrogated it in turns.

The lion asked: "Is there any possible chance for you to escape at our firm grip now?" The sheep replied: "No, I cannot manage it at all to escape from even a single grasp of anyone of you!" "Yes, you are right; you cannot even manage to escape from the claws of my junior cousin, the hyena," the lion narrated.

The lion asked: "Tell us now three fundamentals facts about life that can make us release you freely without being eaten up?" The sheep brightly responded: "Only the God of Heaven and the Earth can touch your hearts so that you can set me freely unharmed." The lion seconded: "Surely, you are right; only God makes such things happen."

The sheep continued to voice his second response: "And if it happens that you could set me free, I tell you, my relatives and fellow human beings will never understand and believe me right when I communicate the information to them!" The hyena nodded: "That's true; they will actually not be-lieve you right, if you could meet them again and say to them that a lion and hyena set me free!"

And the sheep finally concluded by commenting: "If you guys had not eaten any prey since morning, you would have not bothered asking me all these questions!" The two carnivores were im-pressed with the sheep's brainpower and the lion appreciated him so much: "How wise are you? You managed to convince us all." The lion and the hyena finally set the sheep free after the sheep had successfully answered the three ultimate questions well.

# 55

## The Bat's Rejection

The bat woke up one morning to join one of the two distinctive groups of animals and birds that were celebrating their new year's festival. Animals and birds used to celebrate at the end of every year as a sign of thanksgiving function to their supreme deity. The bat first met the animals' group and he was refused since he had wings and two legs which made him qualify to be a bird.

He was then annoyed and hastily left the animals' group and approached the birds' group whose dance was also at its climax. The birds were once again singing some of their below verses which they sang sometimes back during one of their colleagues' marriage competition:

*"Arialbeek: Adhueŋdït kac tuac-tuac cïn köu yuöm töŋ awïl,*
*Jak: Peec xök e wuo cin; guo bieth xoc në dan liac,*
*Awet: Dhɛldït tom rol, jo bɛr yɔk ke yï kääc, cɔk yɛn cɔk dier nya,*
*Dhɛl: Tɛt nyïïr ke wunda, guɔ nhom nyɔt awälɛ,*
*Arumjoh: Ye tuöt xa bɛr lial, cir ke ye xen cok man cɔk kääc ke*
*thon-chieŋ, Mabek!"*

*This is translated as:*

**Saddle-billed Stork** *(Arialbeek): A humble and honest fellow who runs tuac-tuac (movement sound made by creatures without backbones) as he had no single skeleton.*

**Pelican** *(Jak): Our cattle were raided at our very hands; consequently, I bartered a spear with an expectant heifer.*

**Crane** *(Awet): Marabou Stork with a protruding throat, just wait for a while and let me have a dance with the lady.*

**Marabou Stork** *(Dhɛl): The works of our ladies' fine hands instantly transformed my hairstyle!*

**Ibis** *(Arumjöh): Why the wild duck scorns me as if I were the one who advised her mother not to produce with the shortest bull lives at Mabek!*

The birds abandoned their performances after seeing the bat joining them! And they instructed him to go away: "Go away please; you are not one of our members?" The bat asked: "Why didn't you guys kick me out of your last year's celebration?" The master of the ceremony responded: "It's because we have presently known that you don't belong here! You are not our member since you have teeth while we have beaks, you have teats while we do not have teats and you give birth to young ones while we lay eggs; you deserve to quit by now please!"

The bat insisted: "Why don't you need me at this point in time guys, yet I have been flying with you all along? Remember I have been performing with you during your competitive marriages and festivals; what brought about all these seclusions now?" And the master of the ceremony in that due course yelled: "Leave us alone in peace please!"

The bat was disappointed, and he flew away with a broken heart and he isolated himself from meeting anyone among both groups of the animals and the birds; and he preferred to move at night so that he would not come face to face with any fellow of the two groups.

# 56

<hr>

## *The Room Master*

Once upon a time before the animals could separate, the cobra, the tiger and the hyena used to live in one hut. They put up together and shared the cost of their rent. They laid down their rules and regulations so that they could live in harmony.

One day, the tiger put his point of concern clear: "I do not need anyone among you at all to aimlessly stare at my eyes; and if anyone does so, I will immediately fight the instigator."

The second animal to express his point of concern after the tiger was the hyena who said: "Whenever I come into the room late at any time of the night, I do not need anyone to ask me where I had been. And if anyone asks me so, I will fight the questioner."

And the last animal to express his opinion was a cobra who said: "As I reluctantly lie down at my location of the hut, I do not expect anyone of you to step onto me; and if someone does so, I will bite the culprit seriously."

The three animals stayed well for the first five months; however, the three animals afterwards gravely fought each other during a rainy night when the hyena lately returned to their hut and loudly banged the door opened. And the tiger was awoken up and he asked: "Who are you?" The hyena replied: "It's me, the hyena." And the tiger continued to ask the hyena: "Why did you loudly bang the door that way? Why don't you respect others peace of mind? Where had you been until this time of the night?"

The hyena was annoyed, and he immediately abused the tiger: "You are a bad-mannered and a ruthless creature! Didn't I tell you sometimes back that I do not need anyone to ask me where I had been at any time of the night?"

"You abused me as a bad-mannered and a ruthless creature! Which other animal has ever abused me as such!" The tiger roared and moved sluggishly towards the direction where the hyena was standing. It did not even take a second before the two animals could violently knock each other in their petite hut.

To make the matter worse, the two fighting beasts unknowingly stepped onto the cobra in the process of their fight and the cobra reacted fiercely by biting the two animals that were tearing their skin badly with their sharp claws in turns. Consequently, they abandoned their fighting and dashed out of their hut without returning, leaving cobra as the room master.

# 57

## The Payback Deal

It was always something mysterious and frightening to see a lion that has widely opened its mouth, approaching and advancing towards your direction in a middle of a forest where you do not have someone to help you!

A hunter was very confused and ran out of thought when the lion approached him in a densely populated forest where there was no one to protect him. The man came face to face with a beast at a comparable step. After that, the hunter swiftly ran away, and the lion recurrently followed him; the lion ran after the hunter for a quite long time, and it did not stop running after the hunter until he surrendered and waited for the beast.

The lion approached him with his mouth wide open. The hunter looked in and realized that a goat femur bone had stuck between the lion's teeth. The hunter came to know that the lion was not out to eat him but wanted to be assisted by having the stuck femur bone removed.

The man held up his fishing spear by his left hand and boldly approached the lion. He held the lion by his lower jaw and removed the bone that had stuck between his teeth. And the hunter slowly retreated and left the lion relieved and freed after he has finally pulled out the bone. The lion deliberately followed the hunter until he identified his homestead and then after, he went on his way.

One day later, the very lion returned at night chasing a giraffe and jumped onto it in the middle of the compound and left it intact as a gift to the hunter and his family members. Earlier in the morning, the hunter's family members woke up and found a dead giraffe in their compound. They were all astounded as they gathered around to check out what killed the giraffe. With astonishment, it was found out that the giraffe was exterminated by a lion as there were presences of a lion's foot prints around the dead animal. The hunters finally come to realize that the lion had wholeheartedly paid the man back for removing the femur bone that had got stuck between his teeth.

# 58

## The Dog and the Fire

Long, long ago before the man could possess fire, only the giant cobra, *biar* had a fire at his homestead. And h refused to give it out to anyone else. The man and his family members did not use to cook; they used to survive on wild fruits, vegetable and on raw meat. One day, it rained very heavily and the man's cave was flooded with water and the only option was to run out of the cave with his family members to the high grounds in the forest.

And the cold weather outside his cave was very terrible! The man asked his dog: "Since you do run well, can you please go and bring fire for us from the cobra's homestead?" And the dog responded: "Yes, I will try my level best later at late night when he's asleep." The man and his family members were happy and promptly came up with a technique of fastening a fire scooping metal at the dog's tail for him to scoop the fire at the cobra's house as they shivered desperately in a condensing frost.

Afterwards, the dog stealthily approached the cobra's house and luckily found the fatal cobra sound asleep around his fireplace. The dog cautiously walked towards the fire and scooped the glowing fire with his fire scooping object and silently ran away.

On his way, he hit some trees like *akɔ̈y* and *waak* with the burning scooping metal to store the fire in them and to obtain it again through friction whenever the fire he is carrying extinguishes. The dog safely arrived at his master's home and the man and his family members were excited. The fire was instantly lit, and the man started to smoke as his wife cooked their food.

And all the family members finally gathered around their fireplace as they warmed themselves. That was how they survived the cold weather, and the dog became their closest friend. They later started hunting together for wild meat and whenever they killed some animals in the forest, they traced the species of those trees where the dog stored fire in them when he hit them with his fire scooping metal to produce fire through a friction. From that day on, the dog has never abandoned the man's homestead.

# 59

## *The Silly Lion*

Very long ago, a brown lion terrorized all the people of the cattle camps. He had been eating many cows for a long period and was never found when people hunted for him. He isolated the favorite and the best cow or a bull among the cattle whenever they were grazing. This action was taken after the lion has clearly scanned the whole area to ensure that there were no herders around to detect whatever he had plotted to do.

One day, a rabbit was strolling in the woods, where he abruptly met with the brown lion. He curtly shouted to himself: "What a nice brown bull, I'm going to make him my favorite dancing bull; I will take him to the cattle camp this evening." And when the lion heard him, he thought that he had not recognized him, and he pretended to be a bull instead as the rabbit claimed! He calculated his opportunity of eating a healthier cow over there at the cattle camp especially when everyone was asleep.

They then moved to the cattle camp and the rabbit took plaited leather and tied it around the lion who pretended to be a bull and the rabbit pulled him as he sang his betrayal song:

*"Aye we kɔc ke yï wuɔt,*
*Aa ye raan ë cië nin, ke liëp ye yïc ku bë pääc,*
*Yien kië ca jol bëi, jalkë bɛɛr kuɔc looi! Lec aɲuämäm!*
*Mathiäŋ diën cië käke jäŋ thɔl,*
*Tɔ̈ŋ atɔ̈ke yic aduruk!"*


Which is translated as:


*You the people of the cattle camps,*
*If you were sleeping, wake up and lend me your ears,*
*Here I have brought him; it's your chance not to let him go freely again!*
*Him, the curved teeth beast!*
*My brown bull which has finished others' belongings!*
*There is a cool war!*


All the people woke up and they were armed up to their teeth before they could come to confirm what the rabbit was talking about. It did not take a long time before all the youth's spears landed onto the brown lion. The lion tried to fight back but it was too late for him to respond. He only injured a few of the young men before he kicked the bucket. In the end, all the people thanked the rabbit for the job well-done.

# 60

## The Shattered Promise

A grandfather to the gorilla family woke up one day in the morning to collect some fallen wild fruits and vegetables. He woke up earlier that morning because his neighbors had released their goats and sheep into the forest to collect some nice fallen fruits. And he was the first to arrive at the area before the rest.

He faintly heard a lion's voice in one of the nearby well saying: "Who's that moving under the trees; if you have heard me, can you please come on here and pull me out of the well?" He ignored it and continued to move from tree to tree as he picked and ate some fresh fruits.

The old gorilla picked a bitter fruit and abruptly sneezed: *"Oñm! Oñm!"* And that was when the lion came to realize that it was a grandfather to the gorilla's family that was wandering around in the vicinity picking some fresh fruits. And the lion cried out loudly for some help beneath the well: "Grandfather to the gorilla family, can you please come and pull me out of this well!"

The old gorilla came and asked: "If I pull you out of the well, will you not eat me up sir?" And the lion responded: "No! No! No! I will not eat you up please; I will not dare do that my relative. All in all, I assure you please that I will not eat you." And the old gorilla shouted:

"Just wait for a while; I'm rushing home to bring a ladder. And believe me you; I will pull you out of the well right away."

The old gorilla returned carrying a ladder and lowered it straight-away into the well and the lion finally walked out of the well.

And it was something totally strange to hear later from the lion himself that he was very weak and could not manage to go on his way for a hunt unless he ate the old gorilla to gain some strength at least! The grandfather to the gorilla family asked: "Are you aware that promise is a debt! How come again for you to twist the best promise that you assured me of! Are you up to your promise?"

The arguing animals were not aware that their words were also being heard from a far distance. And dozens of animals guided by the fox arrived and the fox asked: "What's all this quarrelling about fellows? Calm down colleagues and let us all just go over there and sit under that tall tree, and I assure you that your case is going to be settled fairly."

They all walked to the tall tree and sat down under its shade as the king of the jungle, the lion was asked to explain what the matter was all about between him and the old gorilla. But he refused to share his views with the animals and when the animals realized that the lion was not in the mood of talking, they asked the old gorilla to explain what the problem was all about. And the gorilla clearly narrated the whole story from the begging up to the end, but all the animals feared the lion.

Snappishly, the fox seized the first opportunity to express his views: "The lion is right; he has spent a couple of days in the well without eating a thing! How would he manage to chase his prey if he has not eaten something! You the monkey should be eaten up right now by the lion before we separate. And the monkey, *tim de kuär nhom ka!*" Which is translated as: *there is up of your ancestral tree.*

No sooner did the fox complete expressing his views than the old gorilla immediately escaped and climbed the tallest tree and swung from tree to tree and all the other animals speedily ran away and they disappeared into the forest leaving the lion in anguish as the deal did not work out.

# 61

***

## *The Rowdy Leader*

L ong ago before the judges took their roles, leaders were the ones who could consider their victims' cases. The frogs did not like their contemporary fellow frogs' leader because of his being dwarf; they wanted a leader whom they would look up in his eyes like a saddle-billed stork, *Arial-bheek*. They eventually called for a meeting and *Arial-bheek* unanimously was elected as their leader. However, *Arial-bheek* liked a frog's meat and things turned out to be devious when *Arial-bheek* swallowed his subjects in broad daylight whenever he's settling their cases. He would quickly swallow two, three or four frogs whenever they presented their cases to him. It was something of mystery; all the frogs that used to go for the hearing of their cases at *Arial-bheek's* home did not come back in the end!

One day, five frogs brought their case of a fight over an insect to him and his crave of swallowing a fat frog dragged him; he swiftly swallowed four frogs but only one frog escaped and he by then hurriedly jumped into a pool of water. The survivor went and informed his fellow frogs that their currently elected leader, *Arial-bheek* had turned out to be a snake; he had swallowed four of their members and he was the only one that managed to escape!

It eventually came into light why their fellow frogs progressively disappeared whenever they went to *Arial-bheek's* home for the hearing of their cases! All the other frogs teamed up and they went to *Arial-bheek's* home. And they found him seated outside his compound waiting for his plaintiffs to come up to him. The frogs came and asked him some few questions at a distance: "Are you really our true leader? If you are, what a leader eats his subjects! Are you still our leader after swallowing our fellow frogs?"

Conversely, *Arial-bheek* aggressively responded: "You are all under arrest," as he slowly approached the army of frogs. He swiftly ran into the group of frogs and started to swallow a few of them and the rest jumped into one of the nearby pools of water. *Arial-bheek* is still pursuing the frogs at the pool where he got hold of a few of them. Up to date, the saddle-billed stork does not want to leave any stone unturned; he's still stalking for the frogs that acutely abused him.

# 62

---

## *The Lost Link*

Back the olden days after a man and a woman were created, the earth was so near to the heaven that people on earth would easily reach God in the sky by a rope that was stretched between the two.

When people were sick, they could climb the rope to the heaven for healing. And when they were old, they could climb it too so that they could be made young again and death was unknown.

One day, a small bird called *atɔc* and its young ones landed besides a mortar, pounding device *(doŋ)* where a woman was pounding some millet grain. They came to pick up some scattered grains that had fallen around *doŋ*. And suddenly, the woman indiscriminately hit the innocent young ones of *atɔc* with a pestle to death.

Without a delay, the mother to the smashed young ones retaliated by cutting apart the rope which was the man's easy access to heaven; the other end of the rope went up while the other end returned onto the ground!

And the great connecting rope was totally lost and there was no other connection between the earth and the heaven as there was no mean of going up to heaven for taking both the sick and the old ones. From then henceforth, the people on the earth lost their link to the heaven and they were exposed to death and sickness.

# 63

<hr>

## Keep an Eye

Once upon a time, a rabbit, and hare and a fox went to visit one of their in-laws. They trekked for quite a long distance before they could reach their destination. On their way, the three animals collected three big shells which they could use as spoons and kept them in their bags. After a while, a fox yelled: "Is it not a shameful act for us to carry these things in our bags while we are visiting our in-laws? Why don't we leave them here and we would then pick them later when we are returning home?"

And when they heard that, the rabbit threw away his and the rest pretended that they had thrown away theirs as well, but they did not. They then reached their in-laws homestead, and they were warmly welcome. And in the evening, the fox reported that their food should be brought to them without spoons. After a while, they were served with a delicious hot food without spoons.

As intended, the hare and the fox removed their shells which were to be used as spoons, but the rabbit felt deeply sorry for throwing away his spoon some hours back!

On a tricky note, the other two animals told the rabbit to return to the site where he threw away his to bring it and his colleagues promised that they would not start eating the food in his absence until he returns!

The rabbit agreed and he quickly pulled out his one eye and placed it at one of the corners of the conical hut where they were seated in to oversee whatever his colleagues would do as he returns where he threw away his shell. And then he left for his shell. As the rabbit was swiftly making his way to the location, his other eye that he kept at the corner of the hut spotted that his friends were about to start eating the food while he was away, and the rabbit immediately reacted: "Hey! Hey! Wait for me colleagues! What are you guys trying to do? Didn't you promise me that you would wait for me until I return and then we would altogether start eating our food?"

The hare and the fox were very astonished how the rabbit could see them yet he is not physically there with them! The rabbit kept on warning them several times whenever they wanted to start eating the food while he was away until he returned. Afterwards, the three animals altogether started eating their delicious food after the rabbit has returned. If the rabbit had not kept one of his eyes at one of the corners of the hut, the fox and the hare would have eaten up all the food before he returned.

# 64

---

## *The Paradox of the Fox*

Previously in the jungle, all the animals except their king, the lion suffered the hunger during summer times after a severe calamity had hit the animals' kingdom; the lion had many sheep and goats. One day, the lion had an announcement when all the animals were present: "Hello folks, I have a healthy sheep that I would give to someone whom I will eat at the fall of autumn, this year. Who would like to have it eaten guys?"

The fox raised his hand and was excused by the lion to air out his opinion. He paradoxically responded: "I'm ready to take the sheep and thankful to our king, the lion for his offer; it is not a big deal, I will eat the sheep and am ready to be eaten up by the lion come autumn this year!"

It was a very great surprise to the rest of the animals why the fox dared make such a deal with their mighty king! The fox took the sheep to his farmhouse and immediately slaughtered it as a great meal for his family members. And he dried three quarters of the meat for his future consumption.

Days just went on fast and the autumn unfolded. Without a delay, the lion early in the morning came to the fox's homestead and reminded him of their deal and the fox simply responded: "Yes, I'm aware of the deal but would wish to urge you to excuse me for a little more time so that I could complete clearing my gardens and to plant a few crops and vegetables for my children whom I shall leave behind."

The lion was convinced with the explanation and later left for his house. After the fox had completed clearing his farms, he planted a variety of crops and vegetables for his children to survive on. The rest of the animals' living conditions deteriorated as they lived from hand to mouth but the fox's family members lived on the sheep's dried meat.

The lion then returned to the fox's homestead after three weeks, and found the fox ready for the deal, but the only thing that he did not do was a handing over note to his elder son who was out of the house for a hunt. The lion assured the fox so that he would return the following day.

That evening, the fox left his house and went into the forest to round up some striped animals namely: zebras, giraffes, tigers and leopards and by the next morning when the lion returned, he was very astounded to see the colored animals pegged down at the fox's compound! And the lion asked the fox: "Why are you keeping all these animals at your house sir?" And the fox replied: "I'm painting them. Would you like your body to be painted as well?" The lion liked the shining striped colors of the animals and he responded: "Yes, I would like my body to be painted too. Would you mind painting me right now?"

The fox replied: "No, I would not mind painting your body right now." And the fox rushed into his house and picked up a very sharp knife which he claimed would be used for painting the lion. He returned and told the lion to lie down. And the lion agreed to lie down while facing up and the fox cut his throat instantly within a second and the great king was finished. The fox immediately called in his sons to come and help him pull away the dead beast out of their compound.

The dead lion lost his wife long ago and only his younger son survived him. The lion's young one was confused as to why his father did not return home on time, when he used to report home before sunset! The next morning, he went out of their house to search for his missing father. At last, he found him dead next to the fox's homestead and immediately concluded that he was assassinated by the fox and his family members.

The young lion tried to ambush the fox but the fox uncovered all his plots. The fox feared his vulnerable ones being murdered by the young lion and thus, he relocated his family members up the palm tree where his family stayed without descending but only the fox himself could come down the palm tree using a long rope when he goes out to look for food. The fox comes and asks for a rope whenever he wants to ascend or descend the palm tree.

After a while, the young lion discovered the fox's deal and he one day arrived earlier before the fox could come and asked the wife: "Can you please lower the rope for me!" And unknowingly, the fox's wife lowered the rope. And after a heavy pull, the wife found out a different animal altogether! And the young lion safely arrived and sat on a branch of the palm tree and within a short time, the fox arrived, and he called: "Can you please lower the rope for me." And his wife lowered the rope. He was pulled up too and was almost shocked when he saw a young lion seated up amongst his family members.

The fox got no time to descend the palm tree and he resorted to greeting the young lion as he handed the meat over to his wife: "Can you please cook this meat right now for our very important visitor, the lion." And he sat next to the lion. The fox afterwards came up with some interesting stories about their relationship with the lion's descendants; he claimed that their great grandfather named Anyieth used to live on their contiguous plains. After engaging the lion's attention, he communicated with his wife through codes to cut the branch the lion had sat on.

The fox continued to engage the lion as he pointed out where they separated with the lion's progenies in the wilderness many years back. And at last, he communicated to his wife with an encryption 'cut it down acutely,' *nyiethë -piny*! And his wife heard him, and she speedily cut the branch where the lion sat on. At last, the lion fell off from the palm tree branch with a great thud.

And thus, the fox immediately descended and killed the unconscious lion. He was freed at last as there was no member among the lion's family member left behind whom he should fear again. Eventually, the fox and his family members relocated from the palm tree to their farmhouse.

# 65

## *The Enticed Fish*

T he lion and the fox had been having many issues for a quite long time. And the lion failed to get hold of the fox after some attempted ambushes at his home. Amazingly, the lion hunted for the fox for three consecutive years. One day, he spotted a fox feeding his big fish at his fishpond. The lion wanted to approach the scene, but the fear raged in him as the fox by then had his wooden gun, *ariεc* with him.

The lion remained hidden in the forest as the fox fed his fish. He secretly communicated with his fish when there was no one around: *"kot, kot, rεεc Awan bär camku läŋ, piate nyintɔk, ye kɔn nyin."* Which is translated as: *get weigh, get weigh, the fox's fish, come out and let us eat some lime tree fruits, and it is all fatty; it is all lipids.* And the fish dashed out of the water promptly and started to eat its provided lime tree fruits. The fox kept on communicating with his fish that way for a long period of a time before the lion gave it a second trial of enticing the fox's largest fish. When the fox was away, the lion came to the fishpond and oddly called: *"kot, kot, rεεc Awan bär camku läŋ, piate nyintɔk, ye kɔn nyin."* But the fish didn't come out because the lion's voice was very strange and hoarse.

The lion ran to the house of the fox's neighborhood, the hare and took him to the fishpond where he instructed him to say: *"kot, kot, rɛɛc Awan bär camku läŋ, piate nyintɔk, ye kɔn nyin."* The hare in the same way said: *"kot, kot, rɛɛc Awan bär camku läŋ, piate nyintɔk, ye kɔn nyin,"* and the fish dashed out of the water and surprisingly, it was then grabbed by the lion and they left with it to their dens where they killed it.

And when the fox returned in the evening to feed his fish, the fish did not come out at all after it was called several times: *"kot, kot, rɛɛc Awan bär camku läŋ, piate nyintɔk, ye kɔn nyin,"* and there was not any response heard when he called his fish five times: *"kot, kot, rɛɛc Awan bär camku läŋ, piate nyintɔk, ye kɔn nyin."*

He afterwards rushed to his neighbor, the dog and asked him who had enticed his fish. And the dog told him that he saw the hare being dragged by the lion earlier this afternoon up to his fishpond. The fox was very annoyed, and he stated: "Hmn! The lions are still following me, but they will learn a lesson that they will never forget!"

The fox went up to the lions' village and over there, the fish was given to their king. And the fox secretly followed the lions and professed that his fish was given to one of the wives to the lions' king. And the lions proceeded for their dances while the fox remained hidden in the nearby bushes around their dens.

The lions' king's wives cut the fish into pieces as the fox watched from afar. And they put the fish into a big saucepan and placed it on a fire. In the evening, there was a ceremony where all the animals went for a party. The fox joined them as well and when the dances were at their climax, the fox secretly entered the compound and carried away the saucepan that contained the fish and carried it away into the bushes for him to enjoy.

He carried the cooked fish deeply into the forest where he ate it until he was satisfied. He afterwards concealed some of the fish in a saucepan over there in the forest and he returned to the lion's homestead where he entered one of the dens to the lions and slaughtered a cub whose mother was out for the dance! He at that time, picked the

biggest saucepan that contained some dried meat, poured its contents
away and placed into it the cut cub's meat soberly and placed it on
the fire again!

The drumming tunes made the animals go on a rampage as the
dance dillydallied. And after the fox had completed his act, he joined
the dancing team once again and happily sang his song: *"Pan de Kɔ̈r
adiër ku tuak mënhden töny, guäk-guäk! Kër Kukuäu. Kër Awan!"* Which
is translated as: *The family members of the lion are dancing while their cub
is boiling in a saucepan!* And the lions suspiciously asked: "What is the
theme of your song fox?" And the fox sang: *"Nyïïr lɔ̈'wut eei luath ke
dhor Majöŋdië, Kërkukuäw!"* Which is translated as: *The ladies going to
the cattle camp, take along with you the switch of my bull, Majok!* And in
a little doubt, the lions thanked the fox for his nice song as they continue with their dances.

The drumming went on and on for hours and when they were
almost ending their festival, the fox escaped into the forest where he
had kept his fish remnants in a saucepan, and he carried it to his residence. After a dance, most the lions were very drunk, and they could
not distinguish that one of their cubs was missing! The lions' king
and his folks sat down after the dances as they wait for their cooked
fish. They were served with their hot stuff and divided the substances
among themselves.

And whenever they give a little meat to their young daughter,
she completely refused to pick it up as she cried out: *"Ya cuët në   yen
adië ku ke menhkäi, dɔ̈ŋ luŋ tɔny, dɔ̈ŋ abek tɔny!"* Which is translated as:
*How do I eat it yet it's my sibling, the jewels and the beads have remained in
the saucepan!* The cub refused to eat the meat, but the lions and lion-
esses unknowingly ate their young one's meat and they didn't bother
to ask the whereabouts of their missing cub and they also did not pay
any attention to recognize whether what they ate was a fish or a meat
as they were all drunk!

At last, they found the rings, *luŋ* and the waist beads, *abek* beneath
the saucepan! That incidence really pained the lions and the lioness
very much. However, the fox was nowhere to be found. Just within

some few minutes, the lioness was dazed and was unconscious for a week after she wept bitterly over the aching death of her cub! The lions regretted it and their king said: *"Në Awan be bɛr bën, ku ba bɛr dɔm!"* Which is translated as: *I wish the fox would come back and I seize him!*

# 66

---

## *The Divide and Eat Tactic*

L ong ago in a grassland, *lɔh,* there lived three bullocks: the white, the red and the black. The bulls escaped from their master, the man and settled alone over there as they ate greener pastures. They collectively stayed for years as they enjoyed some healthier pastures. Whenever the wild animals tried to attack them, they collectively defended themselves by coming together as they faced different directions. Many wild animals monitored their moves days and nights for many months but there was no a single day that the three were separated.

The bulls had sharp horns which gave wild animals' hard times to attack them. During one of their fine days, one of the lions directly approached them and said: "Hello guys, I approached you today to alert you that the other wild animals detect you at night because of the presence of the white bull amongst you. If he's eliminated, the black and the red ones would all have rest; can I please free you guys by eliminating him?"

The red bull answered: "Surely, you can eliminate him; I'm fed up of running around all over the nights!" Just within a short time, the lions speedily jumped onto the white bull after hearing the red bull's responds. The white bull struggled with the lions for a long time, but he did not manage to escape. The lions ganged up and finished the white bull within some few minutes before the rest of the lions could even join the duel.

And afterwards, the two remaining bulls calmly left the scene where their fellow white bull was torn apart by the hungry lions. And shockingly, many more lions followed both the red and the black bulls and one of them told the black bull: "You guys are still being targeted at night by the beasts because of the presence of the red bull. If we can get rid of him, you the black bull will not be a victim anymore. And if we can deal with him right now, you will be more secure, and we will appreciate that!" And the black bull dimly agreed!

The rest of the lions immediately rushed towards the red bull after their member concluded their talks with the black bull. Within a blink of an eye, the lions promptly seized the red bull from behind and the black bull fearfully ran his own way. The lions then finished tearing apart the red bull with the hope of attacking the black bull that has suddenly dashed into the forest. And the red bull was too small to satisfy the starved lions who then completed eating it within a few minutes before they thought of pursuing the black one who had fled the area.

The pride of lions then ganged up for the search of the black bull that fled while they were eating the red bull. It was a tough search and they eventually spotted the black bull in the evening in the woods. The enormous bull saw the lions approaching and started to run for his own safety and after a very long pursuit, the lions finally got hold of him next to the man's residence! However, the black bull was the strongest of all the three bulls; he struggled with the lions for a quite long period of a time before they squeezed the life out of him!

Unity is strength; if the three bulls had unity among themselves, the lions would have not eaten any of their team members.

# 67

## *The Elephant and Camel*

Fox has always been a judicious animal; he met an elephant and told him: "A camel is bigger than you and he wishes to fight you!" And the elephant responded: "You are a liar, there's no animal on this planet that's bigger than me! And if there is any-one, I have no objection of fighting him if he is willing to fight me too." Nevertheless, the elephant was rather curious and nervous too to know that gigantic animal!

On another day, the fox went to the camel's compound and said: "An elephant claims to be bigger than you and he wants to rough shoulders with you if you would not mind!" And the camel replied: "I want to see him first before we could shake our muscles." Both the elephant and the camel did not know each other but they would rather see each other when they fight.

After the fox had known their stands, he invited them to come to his homestead for a duel the following morning. And the camel was the first animal to arrive. And at around quarter past seven, an ele-phant was seen coming from a distance and the fox snappishly called the camel and showed him how the elephant looks like!

It was a great shock altogether for the camel to see the mammoth elephant approaching! And just within that moment, the camel declared his viewpoint: "I will not dare to fight the approaching massive creature! By the way, where will I hide myself so that he should not see me? I do not want him to meet me either."

The fox told the camel to go and lie down behind a heap of sorghum canes, *kuut*. And the camel hastily rushed and hid himself behind *kuut*. And in a while, the elephant arrived and asked where the camel was! And the fox replied: "The camel has just gone to the market to buy some tobacco and he will be back shortly since he has left his smoking pipe behind that *kuut!*" Astonishingly, the fox pointed the camel which was hiding himself behind *kuut* to be the camel's smoking pipe.

However, the elephant moved to an area where he could properly see the said smoking pipe behind *kuut* and unpredictably said: "If that's the camel's smoking pipe, then he must be greater than me and I will not challenge him for a fight somewhat, period!"

The elephant quickly turned back and left the fox standing as he returned to his dynasty. And in the end, the fox joined the camel where he had hidden himself and informed him that the elephant had just left. Nevertheless, the camel loyally accredited both the fox and God for rescuing him from fighting the huge animal.

# 68

*The Brides*

Once upon a time, there lived an old man who was left in poverty by his parents. His father had only a few goats, donkeys and a dog before he died. The old man had only one wife and they were not blessed with a child for two decades after they got married. If the old man had some cows, he would have married a second wife.

His wife was blessed with two boys and a girl when the wife was in her forties. His boys were much disciplined and so was her daughter; the boys were exemplary to their only young sister. After two decades, the old man's hardworking boys and a daughter had enough millet and sorghum to exchange with cows but there was no market for their cereals.

The old man's boys were stressed as they all wanted to marry but their dad had no cows to give as their bride prices. And after a year when his only daughter was up to the age of getting married, three handsome gentlemen from well-known families' backgrounds declared themselves to marry the old man's dear daughter. And the parents together with their children rejoiced for the good opportunity that had befallen their family.

And the normal marriage procedures were followed. At last, each of the three contestant's relatives pledged to give fifty heads of cattle as their bride prices. The youth from the bride's section were sent to the various competitors' cattle camps to ascertain whether the in-laws' said number of cattle were available or not. And in the evening, all the teams reported that the very stated numbers of cattle were all available from each side of the contesting gentlemen.

And after the verification of the said number of cattle, the relatives to the bride came together to ask their daughter and a few of their close relatives whom they would love to choose as a husband to their daughter among the three contestants. It was a tough decision to make and was a kind of a win-win matter where the mother and the father, their sons and relatives were given the opportunity to choose whoever they love most among the three gentlemen to be the husband to their only daughter.

No solution was reached that day as the relatives were disagreeing. And all the relatives dispersed that evening as their discussion was to be continued the following day. And at around five o'clock that evening, the old man did not feel well, and he had to go to his room for a rest.

Over there in his hut, the old man dreamt: "Lock your valued daughter, a donkey, and a dog into your new-built hut for a night and by the following morning, slaughter a goat before you could open the door to the hut." And the old man woke up straightaway! However, he stayed awake for a while before he slept again, and the same dream repeated itself twice. The old man immediately woke up and called all his sons and a daughter and told them what he has been dreaming about three times. His sons and a daughter agreed to lock the young girl into their new hut together with the donkey and the dog for that night.

He did not dream again, and the night passed by and the old man and his sons woke up earlier the following morning and slaughtered a goat before they could open the door to their hut. After the door was opened, the old man and his sons were very astonished to see the three identical girls who completely resembled their only daughter coming out of the hut! The three girls were undistinguishable except for the fact that they missed scars on their foreheads unlike their ordinary sister who has a scare on her forehead as her unique identity feature.

On another hand, there was neither the donkey or the dog left inside the hut! And the old man finally said:"This is a mystery! These are your sisters, my sons from today henceforth!" And just at around nine o'clock in the morning, all the relatives to the old man returned for the continuation of their meeting that was left in suspense the other day and they were later surprised to see the three girls in the compound. And the old man then opportunely narrated the whole story to his relatives.

All the relatives gathered for their consultative meeting after they had some conversations with their new daughters. After their talks with the new girls, the relatives testified that all the girls physically look like their ordinary daughter. Their voices and how they smile was the same, but their attitudes and characters were quite different from their ordinary daughter's traits. Subsequently, the meeting did not last for a long time since they had three girls in hand for the three contestants; each contestant was provided with a girl at their respective cattle camps and their relatives jubilantly celebrated thinking that they had won the actual contested girl!

The old man's relatives shortened their marriage processes by collecting directly all the proposed number of cattle from all the competitors; a total of one hundred and fifty heads of cattle from their three daughters were received. And after a day, a total of six bulls were brought and slaughtered by the three different clans of the bridegrooms for the brides' relatives. And on the same note, the brides' relatives slaughtered some more bulls for the bridegrooms' relatives since slaughtering of bulls is a symbol of sealing the marriages ties.

Just after some few months, the new brides' negative character traits started to show up at their respective homes. Only one among the three brides had human characteristics while the rest did not; the second one had a dog's characteristics while the third had a donkey's characteristics. The two brides with the dog's and donkey's characteristics gave their husbands very hard times as they always caused trouble and havoc while the actual daughter lived a moral life in her marriage.

# 69

## The Times

Once upon a time, an elephant and a dog got pregnant in the same month. Six months down the line, the dog gave birth to six puppies. And six months later, the dog got pregnant again and gave birth to another six puppies. Within a year, she had dozens of puppies in total and the pattern continued.

In the eighteenth month, the dog approached the elephant and enquired: "Are you sure that you are pregnant? We fell pregnant the same month and I have given birth three times and my puppies have now grown big, yet you are still pregnant; what is going on with your child?"

The elephant replied: "There is nothing that is wrong with my child, but you need to understand: 'What I'm pregnant with is not a puppy but an elephant! I only give birth once in two years' time. And when my baby hits a ground, the earth feels it! And when my baby crosses a road, human beings stop and watch it in admiration. What I carry draws attention. So, what I'm carrying is might and great!'"

# 70

### The Help in Return

Once upon a time in the grassland of Pur-rap, there lived different kinds of animals. One day, a rat was darting around playing in the forest. It mistakenly reached the locality where the lion was resting, and it accidentally landed on its back!

The lion was immediately awoken up by the disturbing little rat and it straightaway got hold of the innocent rat. "How dare would you wake me up tiny rat while I was resting!" The lion roared. "I'm sorry my dear, I just landed on your back by a mistake, and I did not intend to wake you up." The rat sincerely begged the lion to pardon him.

"Hey, what if I swallow you right now?" The lion asked. "No please, do not swallow me our king; I will do you a favor one day by helping you out of a problem as a return!" The little rat respectfully stated. "Heee! Hee! This is something very ridiculous! How can a small animal like you help a mega one like me out of a problem? This is totally a white lie!" The lion disputed the rat's statement. And at last, the lion released the rat unharmed, and it finally exclaimed: "Thank you so much the king of the jungle for being that kind!"

The little rat went on his own way and narrated the whole story to his relatives, friends and colleagues after he had reached home, and they were all very appreciative to the kind lion for leaving one of their colleagues unharmed. Some days later, the very rat went very deep into the forest to gather some wild fruits and roots. Unpredictably, the little rat heard a lion roaring in agony in the nearby bushes.

The rat's curiosity took over and he went to the locality where the lion stridently sounded. It quietly approached the scene and surprisingly came to recognize his friendly lion who pardoned him some days back was caught up in a hunter's trap. The rat directly came into sight and assured his friend: "Do not worry my friend; I will help you out of this imprisonment right away!" But this was a sort of disbelief to the caught-up lion.

The little rat made a loud emergency whistling to beckon his relatives and friends to rush quickly towards his direction without a delay. They all heard the call and rushed to the scene. After reaching the site, the rat said: "This is my very friend I described to have pardoned me some days back; kindly let us all help him out of this seizure by breaking apart this hunter's net that has caught him!"

Without a delay, the rats conjointly cut the hunter's net apart and the lion was untied and set free. At last, he was grateful to the little rats for helping him out of the hunter's trap and he finally went on his way.

# 71

---

## *Think Before You Act*

At ancient times, there lived an imprudent young man who terrorized everyone in their village and its surroundings. One day, he planned a terrorizing visit to one of the nearby villages. On his way before reaching the area, he found a human skull. Unpredictably, he trundled it with his sticks and said: *"Ee kë de nhomdu eyen näk yïn!"* Which is translated as: *It was your own thoughts that killed you!* He severely rolled the skull using his stick as he repeated the same statement.

After sometime, he suddenly gave up rolling it and left the territory. No sooner did he turn his back going his way than the skull shouted: *"Ee kë de nhomdu eyen bë yïn nɔk eya!"* Which is translated as: *It is your thoughts that will kill you too!* Surprisingly, he returned to the locality and stood by the skull and unthinkingly asked: "How will my thought kill me?" However, the skull did not respond. After seeing that the skull was no longer interested in responding to his questions, he then abandoned the area and went his own way.

Just after some few steps, the skull shouted again: *"Ee kë de nhomdu eyen bë yïn nɔk eya!"* But he absurdly looked back and continued going on his way. After a mile long journey, he met a troop of soldiers on their mission, and he ordered them to stop and greeted them: "Hello folks! How is your stretched journey? And where are you rocketing to?" All the soldiers stood still in surprise as they gaze at him questioning whether the gentleman was out of his mind or not!

After some few minutes of their talks, he spotted a General amidst the soldiers and he approached him and hailed: "Hello big fish. I found a human skull that speaks over there!" And he pointed where he found it. "Can you all please come with me to confirm it by yourselves?" And the General replied: "How can a skull speak! There is no skull that has ever talked! Please, leave us alone; we are on an imperative mission. You are wasting our time please." However, the gentleman insisted: "Let us go please my people and if this is not true later, you will unquestionably kill me immediately!"

The General agreed: "Okay. Let us go people, since this gentleman knows what he has seen and on the other hand, he has already passed a judgment up on himself."

The soldiers moved with him to the very place. On reaching the scene, the gentleman started to challenge the skull: *"Ee kë de nhomdu eyen näk yïn!"* However, there was no reply that was heard afterwards! And the General interrupted him: "Raise your voice please; maybe it will speak up soon!" The gentleman kept on retelling the same words to the skull but there was no reply at all that was heard then from the skull.

In the end, the General stopped him and asked: "Since this skull is not responding you anymore, what can we do next my friend?" And the gentleman replied: "There's nothing else that you can do but to shoot me in the head!" In conclusion, the General said: "Promise is a debt my friend and your own words have already arbitrated you!"

Without any mercy, the General quaveringly removed his revolver and shot the young man straightaway in the head! And finally, the team left the area and before they could go farther, they heard a thundering voice from the skull: *"Ee kë de nhomde eyen cië yen guɔ nɔk eya!"* Which is translated as: *It is his own thought that has killed him as well.* Surprisingly, the soldiers loaded their guns and left the range tactfully.

# 72

## *The Unclear Trick*

O nce upon a time, there lived a herdsman by name Pech in one of the remotest villages along the Nile. Pech had many cattle and a big garden. He was an industrious man who willfully provided the needs for his family. He had a big cattle barn which accommodated many cattle and a spacious tukul for his family as well.

It rained heavily in one of the finest evenings after all the cattle had returned from the fields. Inside his cattle, there was a heap of burning cow dung in the middle of a cattle barn. His wife sent her first born daughter to collect fire for cooking their family meal from the cattle barn, but her father refused! Within that short period of time, his wife came into a cattle barn by herself to obtain a fire for cooking her family meal but her husband did not change his statement!

The wife came into the cattle barn and found her husband seated beside *gɔl*, heap of burning cow dung and she asked: "Can I please collect fire from the burning heap of cow dung?" And the old man reacted to her statement: "*Dhiën acië niet*" which is literally translated as, '*the burning heap of cow dung is compacted*'. However, he refused his wife to fetch the fire from the burning heap of cow dung.

The wife respected the order and matched out of the cattle barn while unhappy! She nevertheless walked in the rain to the neighborhood to collect fire for cooking her family meal and she eventually collected the fire and returned to her tukul and cooked the food mainly for children and herself excluding the husband. Afterwards, the food was cooked and the wife with her children ate the whole food without providing the head of their household with a little.

After the rain had stopped, the old man walked out of his cattle barn and marched into his family tukul and asked: "I'm almost to retire to bed, 'Noŋ piu *ke dëk?*'" Which is literally translated as: "Do we have the food ready?" And his wife responded: *"Jöh acï tɔ̈c mɛɛc!"* Which is literally translated as: *"the dog has laid on the fire (no food that had been cooked) as there was no fire for cooking the food."*

The old man hit back: "I wished I knew not to prevent my family members from fetching the fire for cooking our food from the compacted heap of burning cow dung!"

# 73

---

## *The Glutton (Kleptomaniac)*

Long long ago, there lived a gluttonous man by name Ghen-ghen. Ghen-ghen was a very lazy soul who did eat and drink excessively. Some years later, a severe famine struck his locality and Ghen-ghen and his family ran out of food.

His wife was a very smart and responsible; she used to sneak out of her family house and go to the lion's homestead and illegally collect some sorghum grain for her family members. She had been accumulating grains for her family members' consumption for months before he asked: "Where did you get the grain from?" And his wife replied: "I dug the grain out of the ground!"

Ghen-ghen quickly responded: "Can we please go to the site to dig out some more grains for us?" And his wife agreed: "Yes, we can go to the site." The couples went to the site and started to dig into the ground. However, Ghen-ghen tremendously dug into the ground and found no grain! Still, his wife secretly dropped some few grains into the dug hole and Ghen-ghen spotted the grains and quickly picked a few and hungrily ate them.

In the end, the gigantic man stopped digging into the ground at sunset and retired to his bed, but he did not find additional grains.

His wife woke up earlier the following morning and pretended to be going for a short call, yet she was heading to the lion's homestead. She was closely watched by her avaricious husband! The husband woke up and followed her into the jungle!

Ghen-ghen followed his wife until they reached the lion's homestead. Fortunately, they did not find any lion in the compound and they proceeded into the tukul to collect more grains. Both partners arrived at the lion's den and entered the *yier* (basket-like-medium for storing grain) to draw out some grains. After, Ghen-ghen's wife drew out some grain for her family and she instructed her husband to leave with her, but he refused since he was not satisfied. However, the wife left her husband eating the uncooked grain and returned home.

After some hours, the lions returned from their hunt carrying a lot of bush meat while Ghen-ghen was still inside the *yier* eating the grain! Then after, the lions started to roast the meat and the hungry Ghen-ghen smelled the aroma of the roasting meat and he mumbled to himself: "*Ya thok! Ya thok!*" Meaning my mouth, my mouth.

However, the lions overheard Ghen-ghen murmuring inside the *yier* and they dashed and opened it! Huh! The lions were categorically shocked as to why the gigantic human could crunch uncooked grain! Luckily, the lions pardoned him to leave while uninjured with a load of grain and he safely reached home with the grain.

He ordered his wife to pour all the grain into a big saucepan and cook them for him at once. He returned to his cattle barn full of cattle as he waited for his sorghum grain which were being cooked. Unpredictably, Ghen-ghen day-dreamt and yelled: "Yes, can I come by now!" But his wife responded: "No! Not now, I will call you when the food is ready!" Ghen-ghen repeatedly asked: "Yes, can I come by now!" But she replied: "No one has called you Ghen-ghen!"

Afterwards, Ghen-Ghen's wife called her husband when she was done with the cooking: "You can come right now Ghen-ghen." And he hurriedly stood up and speedily routed out of the cattle barn. However, he unwittingly collided with the bull's horn and he lost his eye without his consent and he reached where his wife was and hastily crunched the grain.

In the process of munching the grain, he asked his wife: *"Tik ëyɔk?"* Which is literally translated: *'Wife! You got?'* And his wife giggled and questioned: "Why are you bleeding at your forehead! What has hurtled you?" And he replied: "It is not blood but a sweat!" She hastily nodded and kept quite as her husband thoughtlessly grind the grain.

In the end, Ghen-ghen finished eating the grain and came to realize that he had lost his eye! He returned to his cattle barn and found his chopped off eyeball hanging on his bull's horn!

# 74

## The Mongooses and the Hyena

O nce upon a time, the members of mongoose family and the hyena accidentally met in the jungle and the hyena inflexibly ordered the mongooses to stand still in their positions and he rushed to call in his co-players for a meal. However, the mongooses jiggled and obeyed the directives.

Just after some few minutes, the fox appeared from the bush and asked: "You guys look anxious, what is the matter?" The head of the mongoose household responded: "Assuredly, the hyena ordered us not to move anywhere where we are standing!" Judiciously, the fox intervened: "*Yakkë dhäl,* which means are you fools! Go quickly on your ways."

And the fox collected some fur from all the mongooses and ordered them to disappear into the wood with immediate effect, whereas he remained behind molding mongoose-like-shapes for tricking the hyenas before they returned. The fox completed the molding processes, imbedded the fur onto the molds and decorated shapes before he went on his way.

After half an hour, the pack of hyenas impatiently returned and found the molded mongoose-like-shapes in the very locality where they were ordered to standstill. Astonishingly, the hyenas grasped and bit the molded models and they all yelled: *"Thio! Yakkë cath në dël thäär ke we ye tiöp!"* which is literally translated as: 'Alas! You guys stroll underneath the shrubberies, yet you are all clay!'

# 75

## The Disabled Monster

O nce up on a time, there lived a disabled monster at Rong-Ajong. The monster lived in a piece of engraved big wood alongside the path that lead to the big cattle camp that was densely populated by the youth. The monster strategically chose the opened timber where people enter and exit the cattle camp.

Many people that were both exiting and entering the cattle camp were disappearing within those few days as the monster bushwhacked the residents. Nonetheless, this was very shocking as many young ladies and gentlemen were radically lost along the path. The youth met and agreed to carry out a general search to find out where their colleagues were disappearing while on their way home!

The youth eventually found the extraordinary monster late in the evening in an engraved wood and it was a terrifying occurrence for the youth to see such a frightening creature! Only the upper part of the beast was seen while its lower part was placed in the carved wood.

Within those few minutes, the beast thundered: "Mine oh! Mine oh! It is a requirement for me to eat the heaviest young man among you without a letdown!" The youth were terrified, and they blindly gave him the heaviest gentleman for him to eat and they all ran away back to the cattle camp.

The monster completed eating his prey and he happily roared severely that evening as he celebrated his utmost time well spent! Nevertheless, the monster regularly continued to ambush and eat the residents of the cattle camp as they used the path since everyone was too horrified to face him.

The monster spotted many girls going back to their homes, summoned them and chose to eat the most beautiful girl among them: "Come along my beautiful prey!" And the lady refused to join the beast inside his carved wood.

By chance, the youngest lady among the girls sneaked out of the group and ran back to the cattle camp. She swiftly went and clearly cried: "The monster has ambushed our sisters on our way home and he has threatened to eat the most beautiful girl among them!" Everyone heard the information and on a specific note, the boyfriend to the most beautiful lady in the cattle camp wisely assumed that it was his wife-to-be that was the victim.

He hurriedly put together his fighting tools and lonely ran towards the said direction. Conveniently, all the other young men followed him. He reached the scene and the girls shrieked when they saw him. The young man bravely assaulted the monster and speared him in the eye, and it sprang out of the carved wood and darted on the ground like a ball. Opportunely, all the youth arrived and came to know that the monster could not support himself firmly as he was incapacitated: "*Acie kë noŋ ye thar!* (The beast had no lower part of his body!)" After seeing that, all the young men collectively joined hands and fought the beast and they simply killed him within a few minutes.

# 76

## The Stabbed Ogre

In the past, men eaters were in abundance before the introduction of guns. One dark night, an ogre stealthily came and eavesdropped at a doorstep while the family members were sleeping. The entrance was tightly closed with interweaved strong grass intruded to form a door to the hut which had minute windows. The ogre could overhear a woman breathing heavily but did not perceive any presence of a snuffling man in the tukul!

The ogre determinedly clutched the interweaved door and hardly pulled it and he could not manage wrenching it! The beast repeatedly pushed and chucked the intervened door, and the head of the family woke up quietly, seized his spears and walked towards the doorstep.

The beast forcefully tried again to break into the tukul and the father to the kids speared the ogre at his upper body through the intervened door and the beast misleadingly alleged: *"Raan yin thany meric!* Which means: Human, you are thrusting in vain!" And the head of the household: *"Athany arunnen!* Which means I will thrust it until dawn!" And the beast quaveringly tossed itself into the air and dashed away in agony. And that was how the household members were freed from the deadly beast.

# 77

## The Smelted Anchor

Once upon a time, there lived many varieties of wild animals in the land of Rong-Akoon. These wild animals threatened human settlements and they resorted to settling in groups. The wild animals frequently broke into cattle barns and ate their domesticated animals. The inhabitants developed their scoping mechanisms. One of the inhabitants of Rong-Akoon went to their local blacksmith to be smelted an anchor (*lieny*).

His *lieny* was then smelted and he paid back the blacksmith with seven gallons of sorghum grains and he eventually collected his protective tool and returned home while happy. He did not sleep in his hut that night but opted to sleep inside his cattle barn to protect his cattle from attack by the wild animals. However, none of the wild animals came to attack.

On one of his sleepless nights when he was guarding his cattle from the pride of lions, the old man overheard the sound of approaching animals' footsteps towards his cattle barn. And he immediately woke up and gathered his fighting tools of which *lieny* was the prime tool for the battle. Besides, his *lieny* was fixed to an extended rope that was tied to a strong lumber.

Suddenly, the wild animals jointly mounted onto the cattle barn and mutually uncovered the upper part of the cattle barn. In the process of removing the thatching grass, the owner of the cattle barn spotted one lion that was almost to enter the cattle barn and he keenly aimed at it and hit it on the forehead until *lieny* penetrated its skull.

The victim screamed out in anguish and the other lions promptly stopped entering the cattle barn and they rushed to check on their pierced colleague! After their thorough examination of their stabbed colleague, one of their experienced associates drew a conclusion: *"Ekennë, ekë bäär thar, ku lën cië thɔɔ̈r ekë logetet, acie bɛɛr piir!"* Which literally means: 'This is a terminal thing! Any animal that is hit by it will never ever survive!'

No sooner did the experienced lion gave his last statement, than the pride of lions ran away leaving their colleague shrieking for help. He kept on crying till dawn when the neighbors came to the scene to witness the episode. In the end, the crowd that had converged at the scene collectively killed the stabbed lion the following morning.

# 78

## The Eaten Brother-in-Law

In the ancient time near the Nile, there lived a python, a fox and his sister, the tortoise. They were living together as great in-laws. The python and the tortoise loved each other so much and had a cordial relationship with his in-law, the fox. The fox and the python communally owned many cattle, and they looked after them in turns day after day.

It normally rained cats and dogs whenever it was a fox's turn to take the cattle to the grazing fields and on the other hand, it did not rain when it was the python's turn to shepherd the cattle. One day, it was the fox's turn to take the cattle to the grazing field, it rained heavily before he returned home with the cattle and he did not cope with the unfriendly weather.

He then returned home and found out that the python had coiled himself around their fireplace as usual! Whenever he moved to find another location for him to settle and warm himself, the python was found everywhere, and this irritated the fox to an extend of plotting an evil deed against his beloved in-law.

It was the python's turn to take the cattle to the grazing field the following day when the fox's annoyance was at the climax and he sharpened his fighting tools for cutting his in-law into pieces. In the evening, the python returned from the grazing field and they slept as usual as it did not rain. It was the fox's turn the next day to take the cattle to the field and it rained worryingly as normal and the fox trembled until he returned home.

No sooner did the fox returned home and found the python in his usual location around the fireplace, than he wordlessly withdrew his sharpened tools and cut the python's long figure into chunks! Thereafter, he wholly placed the portions into the fire for roasting. He did not confide in his sister, the tortoise about the plot. After a moment while his portions were being roasted, he went out and misinformed his sister not to enter the cattle barn as the taboos spell that when the husband is in coma, the wife normally stays away until he recovers.

He returned to the cattle barn where he left his in-law's corpse being roasted! Besides, he confronted his sister and received their food at the entrance of the cattle barn from her as soon as possible to prevent her from seeing her sick husband in accordance with their traditional norms.

The fox ate both their food and the python's roasted carcass over the night. He completed eating the python's meat and he was wondering how he would relay the terrible information to his sister. Nevertheless, the fox cunningly arranged the python's backbones in the heron's (*Alak*) nest on a tree beside the cattle barn.

Earlier the following morning, the fox woke up and loudly cried in pretense until his sister hurriedly jumped out of her tukul to instigate what the matter was! And the fox exhibited the arranged bones to his sister. The widow bitterly cried out in grief while the fox traced where the arranged bones ended.

Unfortunately, the arranged bones ended up at the heron's entrance! And the fox yelled out in a baseless anger as he called his sister to come and witness by herself where the python's skull was laid. Scarcely had the tortoise reached the heron's nest when the fox grabbed the innocent heron by his neck until it overstretched and that why the heron has a long neck!

# 79

## The Hopeless Man

During one of the catastrophic and devastating eras, there lived a helpless man with his wife. They were living in the up-country from hand to mouth and the inhabitants of the area were severely affected by the famine as resources were very scarce and the only available means of survival were wild leaves, fruits and roots.

They then depleted the available resources and people resorted to be helped by their relatives who lived in faraway villages. One evening, several days after they had no food, members of their family sat around the fire to pass their miserable time.

In the process, the man dosed off and almost placed his mouth into a blaze of fire! And his wife intervened: *"Wun-mïth, yïn bë yithok cɔk nyuɔ̈p!"* which is literally translated as: *'the father to my children, your mouth will get burned!'* Ridiculously, the desperate husband replied: *"Ye thoŋ ban ŋo cam!"* which is literally translated as: *'What will I eat with the mouth!'*

In their continuous talks, the wife suggested: *"Toicda acë nyaai ku wän-määth ale bë reec bëi,"* which is literally translated as: *'our swamp had recently got plenty of fish and my brother might bring us some fish.'*

And he unreasonably responded: *"Te ciek toic nyai, ke bë nyaai ne diiŋ ciëkke kuith kɔ̈ɔ̈th?"* which is literally translated as: 'Even if the swamp recently got plenty of fish, would it also produce some roasted spiny eels (*diiŋ*)?'

No sooner did their to and fro conversation end, than the brother-in-law arrived carrying some roasted fish and he could not believe his eyes when he was served with some roasted fish.

# 80

## The Rewards for the Curious Fox

The fox took off to his sister's village and stayed with her for a quite long time before he voluntarily left for his home. His darling sister was married to a devil. He became a close friend to the in-law who trusted him so much because of his intellect attitudes.

One day, the devil secretly invited the fox for cattle rustling at a faraway village. Their food then got finished on their way and the devil resorted to perform his own miracles. The devil spotted a bala-nite tree some yards away and magically ordered the tree to produce some ripe fruits instantly. And he then instructed the fox to go with him to the site and indeed, they found a lot of fallen off balanite tree's fruits lying vulnerably on the ground and they ate them hungrily until they were all satisfied.

The two energic animals then embarked on their long journey and they opportunely covered a long distance before they rested once again. As they were resting, the devil removed his own calabash, placed it on the ground and positioned into it an eating shell (thial). Astonishingly, a food mystically emerged within the calabash until it was filled up to its brim! And they enjoyed eating the strange food.

They then continued with their journey after they completed eating their food.

Just after some hours, they found herds of cattle unattended and they immediately rushed, gathered and chased the cattle towards their village. Luckily, the owners of the stolen cattle did not pursue their raided cattle. On their way home, the cattle plus the raiders were thirsty and the devil performed another miracle of which he up-rooted some elephant grasses (awaar) and adequate water oozed out plentifully and the thirsty animals quenched their thirst.

They then reached home at noon and the fox found the devil's children going to swim at their nearby river and he willingly joined them for the leisure time. They reached the river, and they swam for hours before the devil's children could remove their intestines for their general cleanliness! The fox also asked for his intestine to be removed and got clean as well like his nieces' and nephews' intestines. His intestines were removed, and they continued to swim until an unexpected heavy rain started to pour in! The devil's children rushed for stomachs, but the fox forgot to collect his in the process as they return home.

They all ran home while being rained on until they reached house. The devil's children realized that their maternal uncle did not come with his stomach and one of them asked: "Where is your stomach uncle?" Unexpectedly, the fox came to realize that he had forgotten his intestine at the riverbank and he rushed to the very site in the rain and his nephews and nieces followed him as well. They reached the site and found out that the fox's intestines were eaten up by some black ants (achuk).

The devil's children subsequently found the fox's forgotten intes-tines shredded by the black pants and regrettably, they were unsuc-cessful to put the torn intestines together. Only the fox's large intes-tine was recovered intact, and it was in the end placed back into his abdomen and that is why the fox lacks small intestines and has only an elongated large intestine in his digestive system; and the fox became a mockery of his in-laws! He finally returned home with the rest while very unhappy.

On another note, the fox made up his mind to go for cattle rustling by his own and he woke up earlier the following morning and marched out of the house and set off for his journey. He walked for hours and when he was very hungry, he expectantly walked to the balanite tree where they picked a lot of fruits to collect a few of the ripe fruits but he did not find any fruits.

He proceeded with his journey and he finally found many cattle grazing unattended, and he then rushed and rounded them up and chased them across the fields. Subsequently, the herders saw him running away with the cattle and they seriously ran after him. He was then captured and bitten badly after a long chase and was then left unconscious.

The fox became cognizant at midnight, and he woke up and found his way out of the deadly zone to return home. The fox's life became miserable when he was returning home. He removed his calabash, placed eating shell into it but there was no food that emerged within it. He then packed his calabash and continued with his journey. The fox became very thirsty and when he pulled out some elephant grass to fetch some water to quench his thirst, there was no water that oozed out. However, the fox continued with his journey and he finally returned home in the evening while very tied and he immediately retired to bed. And these many unsuccessful attempts and trials gave the fox a sleepless night.

Everyone woke up the following morning and the devil ordered every man in his house for the mudding of his divine house with simsim. And the rule of the work was that: 'No one should eat the simsim that was being used for mudding the sacred house!'

The fox at that time joined the laborers at work. Nonetheless, the controlling aroma caught his nose, and he was tempted to put a little simsim into his mouth. Unfortunately, his hand instantly got stuck in his mouth and he could not manage to remove his figures within his mouth. The mudding team then called in the devil to remove the fox's hand from his mouth. And in the end, he was set free and warned once again not to repeat the similar mistake.

After the team had completed their assigned tusk, the devil ordered his wife to put a frying pan on fire to generate some oil for cooking the teams' food. And when it became extremely hot, the devil placed his feet into it and a clear oil was produced. Then, their meal was cooked, and everyone got served. In the end, the fox became a laughing stock of the week and the shame dogged him until he could decide to leave the devil's homestead for his home. And he was finally pardoned to leave for his home, and he eventually left for his home.

The fox safely reached his home and found all his family members doing well. The fox reached home that evening and ordered his wife to put a frying pan on fire to imitate what the devil did at his house whenever he needed an oil for his meal and his wife did it so as she was told. After the frying pan had become extremely hot, the fox went near it and place his feet into it the same way the devil did it. Unpardonably, the hot pan severely burned his bare feet and he regretted so much for undertaking that poor decision!

# 81

## *The Widow's Prayers*

During one of the severest calamities, there lived a peasant widow who had neither a close relative nor an acquaintance to give a hand for her survival. She only lived on some strange wild fruits, leaves and roots.

The rare leaves, fruits and roots got depleted and the poor widow stayed indoors for couples of days without food to eat. One night, she earnestly prayed to God for help and amazingly, her prayers were answered when the deity opened the roof of her tukul and placed into it some basic needs as follows: sorghum, beans and ghee in good quantities until her house was filled up leaving only the space where she was sleeping in.

Earlier the following morning when she woke up, she was surprised to see plenty of edible food arranged in her empty tukul! After she had realized that her prayers were answered, she instantly knelt to glorify the Almighty God for answering her prayers. She then invited her neighbors into her house to witness the provided gifts by themselves. She at that time cooked enough food for her neighbors and herself as a gratitude. And after the neighbors were done with their meal, the invited guests ultimately dispersed and recited the widow's miraculous gifts to their colleagues who did not attend.

# 82

---

## *The Forgetful Husband*

A t one of the villages that was torn apart by poverty, many people were disadvantaged, and they lived from hand to mouth. In one of the households, there was a two-year-old boy who lacked something to eat. One night, a father and a mother to the child met and concluded that their son would be taken to his grandmother's home.

The man dressed up his son and they both took off that morning to take his child to his grandmother's home. On the way, the man found many youths from the nearby cattle camp on their fishing expedition. He placed down his child and joined the fishing youth. In the process, the man managed to kill many fish and he was overwhelmed.

The time passed by very quickly and the youth stopped the fishing voyage in the evening, and they left to their cattle camp while the man outwardly collected his fish and left his young boy by the fishponds. He walked back home carrying his many fish and his wife assumed that her husband had taken her boy to his grandmother' home as specified.

He handed over the fish to his wife who afterwards cleaned and cut them into pieces before she could cook them. His wife then cooked the fish, and she served her husband with the hot stew. And after they had finished eating the fish, they retired to their bed. And they conversed for a little while before they could sleep. During their talks, the wife asked: "Did the grandmother to the child felt so happily when you took our child to him?" Wonders shall never end! The man speedily woke up and dashed out and headed where he left the child.

He then reached the fishponds but he could not find his child. Still, an idea kindled in him and he rushed to the nearby cattle camp. He went and asked the inhabitants: "Hey! Did anyone collect my child at the fishpond?" And everyone who heard him chanting laughed ironically.

Luckily, a good Samaritan came to him carrying his child and he was extremely excited. He grabbed his child and spitted onto his head severely to cleanse him.

The father to the child then proceeded with his journey of taking his child to his grandmother's home overnight. He then reached the intended home and woke up the mother-in-law to handover the child and she got up swiftly and asked: "Are you all doing fine at home?" And he answered: "Yes, we are all doing well." It was a great surprise why the in-law walked over the night with the young child! No sooner did the father to the child take his dearest boy to his grandmother, than he requested to return home and he was acquitted to return.

And the father to the child continued with his return journey and he finally reached home at the cracking of the dawn. After reaching home, he found his infuriated wife awake and she asked directly: "Where did you leave our child?" And he lamentably replied: "Sorry to say my dear, I forgot our child at the fishpond and I just took him overnight to his grandmother's home!" And his wife inquiringly questioned: "What made you forget the child at the fishpond?" However, her forgetful husband had no answer to give but to murmur instead!

# 83

<hr>

## The Bird's Nest

Long time ago, there lived a most respected elder in the community. The village was named after his own name as he had many cattle, big gardens and many wives who gave birth to many children.

One day, the famous elder decided to invite his fellow elders to his home after he had updated his family members about his plan.

His wives and children started to put their things in order before the elders' invitation date approached. The following morning, women cleaned the compound, and all children were told to collect and arrange the cow hides (leathers) and papyrus mats for seating the visitors. And the women and the children did it as they were told.

On the very day for the occasion, the visitors started to arrive one by one to the compound and they found their places already arranged as the rest of the visitors were being waited on.

After everyone had arrived, the elder who invited the people stood up, greeted and thanked everyone who had heard and showed up for his invitation. He started to introduce why he invited his fellow elders by pointing at the bird's nest up the tree and he asked the guests: "What is the name of that thing on the tree?" And the guests answered: "*Ee hönnë dit*," which is translated as, 'It's a bird's nest!' He continued to ask his fellow elders: "What if it wasn't a bird's nest, what would it be?" After the guests have keenly heard all this nonsense, they were very annoyed, and they started to leave the compound one by one.

# 84

---

## *Who Can Bell the Cat?*

Long ago in the jungle, there lived a plague of rats in the woodland. And they were much terrified by the cats as they continually consumed their fellow rats.

One day, they realized that they were almost to be finished by the cat and they finally convened a meeting in which its agenda was: 'What should we do to avert these frequent losses of our colleagues' lives by the cats?' Apart from other suggestions, the rats unanimously concluded that they would bell the cat so that they should be able to hear it when it approaches.

And one of the rats' eldest stood up and posted a question: "Who can volunteer to bell the cat amongst us?" In the end, no one volunteered amongst them to bell the cat.

# 85

---

## The Lost Needle

I n the land of birds, the hen and the kite bird *(achuil)* were very great
friends. They were staying together in the same compound. They
used to share their common commodities in their spacious compound. Their chicks enjoyed their amusing times as they played together.

One day, the hen realized that some of her feathers were loose and
they needed to be mended but she had no needle. So, she decided to
ask her friend to offer her a needle if she has any. Luckily, her friend
gave her needle. Later, she then mended her loose feathers, and she
flew low as she tested her fixed feathers.

Some days later, the kite bird came and asked for the needle, but
the hen could not recall where she had placed the borrowed needle!
The kite bird became very annoyed when she heard that her only
needle had been lost and she persistently asked:"Where did you place
my only needle?"And the hen replied:"I will fetch it in the garbage."
But the hen could not find it.

The next day, the kite bird angrily came back and asked again:"Did
you get my needle?" However, the hen uncompromisingly replied by
scratching the garbage and the kite bird did not wait the outcome of
her search, but she forcefully snatched one chick as a compensation
for her lost needle! And that was the genesis of the current conflict
between the hen and the kite bird.

# 86

*The Cunning Hare*

In the oldest days, there lived a cunning hare in the savanna land. The hare spent some days without food. One day, he decided to go out to the woodland to look for something to eat.

While he was strolling in the forest, a crow carrying a fresh meat flew above him and perched on one of the nearby trees. At that point, the hare nicely started his appreciative conversation by describing what the crow's beautiful colors look like!

In the process of their talks, the hare said: "You are such a very beautiful bird with a white color around the neck and the only doubt about you is that I have never ever heard you crowing!" No sooner did the hare sweet-talk the crow, than the crow crowed, and its meat fell out from its mouth!

Swiftly, the hare grabbed the meat and yelled back to the foolish crow: "Do you think I had never ever heard you crowing as you fly all around? My friend, I only wanted to own your fresh meat!"

# 87

*The Foolish Crow*

Once upon a time, there lived two friendlies crows: the pied crow (gang arol) and the black crow (gang col). The two birds built their nests along the River Nile. They spent most of their social times together.

One day, as they were narrating their fabulous stories on numerous wars which their ancestors had fought, the crows eventually came to disagree on whose ancestors were more brave than other one! After their long hot debate, the black crow blindingly put forward a suggestion: 'If you thought we are all brave enough, then why would we not kill our mothers!' And the pied crow sarcastically agreed, and the two birds parted ways to accomplish the mission of killing their mothers.

The black crow then rushed home and foolishly killed his innocent mother on spot while the pied crow did not kill his dear mother. After the black crow had killed his mother, he flew to his friend's home to confirm whether he had killed his mother or not! The pied crow immediately saw the black crow approaching and he gave him a warm welcome.

And the two friends then resumed their normal conversations. Out of the black crow's surprise, the mother to the pied crow came out to greet her son's visitor! No sooner did the black crow saw the pied crow's mother, than the black crow angrily asked his friend: "Why is your mother still alive yet we all agreed that we would kill our mothers to prove our bravery?" And the pied crow replied: "You are just a fool, how dare could you kill your own mother out of a mere joke?"

The black crow speedily jumped towards the pied crow and uncompromisingly grabbed him by his tongue and cruelly pulled it out and the two friendly birds immediately became rivals. And that was how the pied crow lost his tongue.

# 88

## How the Hyena Became Lame

Long ago in the earliest days, the hyena and the fox were great
friends. They were living in one of the thickest jungles. One
day, when they were hunting in the forest, an odor of cooking
ghee caught their attention, and they immediately ran towards the
direction where the aroma was coming from!

They finally found it out that the ghee was being cooked at a
human home by a woman. Over there, the fox instructed the hyena
to go and hide himself in a heap of firewood in the compound as he
would sneak into the house where the ghee was being cooked to steal
it. And he eventually made it into the house and found the warmest
ghee beside the cooking one. And then, he swiftly picked an eating
shell of which he scooped into his gut the warmest ghee three times
before he could carry a spoonful of ghee for his friend who was hiding himself in the heap of firewood.

And the fox stealthily carried the warmest ghee to his friend, and
he whispered: "Take it very quickly and return the eating shell to
me to fetch more ghee for you." The hyena hastily gulped it down
and returned the said tool. The fox sneaked again into the house and
collected more ghee for his colleague, and he came back carrying

the stuff. Unfortunately, the hyena hungrily swallowed the shell. And when the fox asked him to give him back the shell, he whispered: "It has gone with the ghee!"

Consequently, the fox became very furious after their only eating shell was swallowed by the hyena! The fox decided to betray the hyena by disclosing his friend's hideout to the woman: "The hyena has hidden himself in the heap of firewood waiting to steal your cooked ghee!". And the woman did not ignore the information and she went to the site straight away and disassembled the heap of fire until she could spot the hiding hyena and strike the hyena two times at the joint of his femur bone in the process of escaping the woman's wrath. In the end, the hyena eventually managed to escape; but to his misfortune, his femur bone was badly fractured and that was how the hyena became lame!

# 89

―――⊙⦿⦿⊙―――

## The Ogre and the Kind Girl

housands of years ago, there lived a pastoralist with his family in one of a less populated village. They had many farm animals: herds of cattle, goats, sheep and chicken. And his normal routine was to look after the cattle. His nomadic pattern was dictated by the availability of both water and green pastures.

One day as he was looking after his cattle, an ogre changed himself into a spotted bull and joined the herd of cattle. After a while, the shepherd wondered where the bull came from but did not chase the strange bull away from his cattle until he returned his cattle home. After they had reached home, the cattle detected the striped bull's awful smell, and they all ran away leaving only his two bulls. The shepherd's two indigenous bulls confronted the strange one and bitterly fought it and the shepherd liked his bulls' action and did not revoke them as they dealt with the peculiar bull. And the sympathetic daughter to the shepherd innocently intervened and separated the antagonistic bulls.

After the bulls' fight had subsided, the shepherd gathered his cattle into his cattle barn, the spotted bull included. Overnight, the owner of the cattle came to conclude that the presence of the strange bull among his cattle had become an issue, and therefore, he planned to take his herds to the nearby cattle camp for safety the following morning. However, the shepherd secretly left with his cattle earlier the morning, leaving the strange bull and his beloved daughter behind!

When the daughter woke up, she found out that her beloved father had left with their cattle to cattle camp and left her alone with the strange bull! Nonetheless, the strange bull changed into its normal state to be an ogre and the poor girl quickly put her two gourds which contained ghee and milk respectively into a traditional-child-carrying-basket (*diony*) and swiftly took to her feet and the ogre ran after her and sang his song:

*Akon yɔn bie wuur yɛn!*
*Ku ye yɛn cɔk nëk thɔn!*
*Cok yɛn cɔk nëk adhuek ke wunden eeh!*

Which is literally translated as:
*Akon, when your father brought me!*
*And he let me be beaten up by his bulls!*
*He let me be beaten up by the young bulls eeh!*

*And then Akon broke into her own song:*
*Jo wäär yɛn maan!*
*Jo yen nyaŋ kɔr Makuac!*

Which is literally translated as:
*Then my father hated me!*
*He left me to the spotted ogre!*

*And the ogre retorted:*
*Ku ja yin cam ŋo?*
*Yin nyan waan ye ya kony ne thɔn.*
*ŋo cin yɛn yin tok ku ba ben juatic!*

Which is literally translated as:
*Why should I dare eat you?*
*You the very girl that did save me from the bulls.*
*Why can't you give me one to lick into it?*

The girl then dropped a gourd that contained ghee to the ogre and the monster at that moment stopped and consumed the ghee while the girl kept on running.

The beast hungrily completed eating the ghee and quickly resumed chasing the miserable girl. No sooner did the girl saw the ogre approaching her, than she dropped another gourd that contained milk towards the ogre, and she kept on running; and the ogre stopped once again to consume the content in the gourd.

The ogre finally completed ingesting the milk and quickly ran in pursuance of the girl. The young girl saw the ogre approaching and she immediately dropped the traditional-child-carrying-basket that contained some dry meat to the beast, and she kept on running. The ogre then stopped and completed eating the dry meat and continued chasing the empty-handed victim.

The poor girl yelled out for help and luckily, her shrieking voice was heard by the youths at the cattle camp. Luckily, the young men picked their fighting tools and ran towards the direction where the voice of the crying girl was heard. They abruptly met the poor girl almost to be caught by the ogre and they aggressively confronted the beast and speared him to death.

After the youth had killed the ogre, they returned to the cattle camp with the rescued girl who afterwards disowned her father for leaving her with the ogre! The girl was highly welcomed by her relatives and friends with their hands opened. And she slept for many hours until the following morning when their anger with her father was settled by her uncles. During their talks, her father apologized for leaving his daughter unattended and he was forgiven by his daughter for the unfortunate decision.

# 90

## The Made-Up Demise

Once upon a time, there lived a tricky and a selfish fox with his relatives. He had big gardens planted with beans, sorghum and maize. He also had beehives. During one of the finest seasons, he harvested plenty of his farm produce.

After seeing that he had enough farm produce, he selfishly thought of consuming them alone by denying his relatives from enjoying the fresh farm products! He made a self-centered plan by digging a tunnel from the forest till his parental home and carried into it all his farm produce.

A day later, he went into the forest and purposely ate variety of fruits, roots and honey to upset his stomach. In the evening, an uproar from his stomach started and his parents were all puzzled! However, he kept on eating those wild fruits and spent sleepless nights complaining of his continuous stomach discomfort.

One day, he called his parents and relatives and dropped a bomb shell that his time to die has finally come because of his internal organs malfunctioning! This bad news truly shocked his kinsmen. He suggested that his grave would be dug within their compound. The idea sounded sarcastic and parallel to their customs that no grave is dug before anyone dies! He insisted and opted to dig his own grave by himself! And it took him two good days to complete digging his own grave and covered it with mud leaving only his own entrance.

He gathered all his relatives and friends to bid them final adieu and finally entered his spacious grave. The cunny fox then connected his grave with the tunnel where he had kept his farm products. And after he had completed connecting the two burrows, he sorted his belongings into types and he could prepare and enjoy his meals. As he was cooking his beans inside his grave, the boiling pot produced some sounds that was heard by his relatives outside his grave and his mother exclaimed: "My son's stomach is right now getting burst!"

The fox enjoyed staying within the cave until his commodities got finished and he eventually came out of the grave and claimed to have recovered while inside the grave! And this was a kind of a disbelief by both the fox's family members and the villagers; and it became the talk of that month.

# 91

## The Shattered Friendship

In one of the biggest cattle camps, there lived a lady by name Nyijiny with her brother, Deng. Deng also had his namesake as a friend. They did dance together, and he had a good–looking colobus monkey's dancing hide (aga –rial). One day when they were about to migrate to another cattle camp, the two friends' *agaŋ-rial* were given to Nyijiny who afterwards forgot them in her temporary hut (*dul*).

After a long day walk, they finally reached the destined cattle camp and got settled. Four days later, a dance was organized by the youth, and before the dances could start, the two gentlemen went to Nyijiny to collect their *agaŋ-rial*. However, Nyijiny came to release that she had forgotten the *agaŋ-rial* at the abandoned cattle camp. And she passed the unpleasant information to her brothers and that aroused Deng's friend's disappointment.

Deng's friend insisted that he wanted his very *agaŋ-rial* even though it had been forgotten at the abandoned cattle camp! Their age mates intervened by trying to persuade him but he kept on demanding Nyijiny to give him his *agaŋ-rial!* Nyijiny's brother suggested to give his friend two bulls in compensation for the forgotten *agaŋ-rial* but his friend could not accept the offer. After a thorough thought, Deng suggested that he would compensate his friend's dancing hide with all his cattle instead of either his beloved sister or himself would embark on the insecure journey of returning to the abandoned cattle camp to check on their forgotten *agaŋ-rial,* however, his friend turned down the second offer!

Nyijiny took inappropriate decision overnight out of her guilty conscience that she would return to the abandoned cattle camp to fetch the forgotten *agaŋ-rial!* She safely reached the abandoned cattle camp the following morning and she got the two *agaŋ-rial* in their good conditions inside the *dul.*

And she then left the *dul* after she had collected the *agaŋ-rial.* And after a few yards from the *dul,* the pride of lions and a pack of hyenas emerged and started to chase the helpless girl who then broke into a song:

*Yen yuop lɔ̈r kiyee,*
*Yuop yen abeth ke thiaŋ,*
*Ago cie dan cie rot pet ne weŋic!*

Which is literally translated as:
*Here I beat this drum,*
*How I beat the little ones of thiaŋ,*
*Until it looked like a stretched calf inside a cow!*

And the pride of lion sang their song:
*Ku cam ŋa?*
*Ku cam Nyijiny,*
*Ye Nyijiny nyän yïndië?*
*Ee nyan pieth awään,*
*Yennë ka cië keech yupic!*
*Tim ye waak, tim de akɔ̈y, tim cie gääl!*

Which is literally translated as:
*And who can I eat?*

*And I can eat Nyijiny,*
*How does Nyijiny look like?*
*She is the incredibly beautiful lady that was here,*
*She is the one that had beaten a newly embossed drum!*
*The tree of waak, the tree of akɔÿ, a tree that does not bend!*

And the pack of hyena sang their song too:
*Aguek-yaar! Aguek de wën wäh!*
*Ɣeer puot, puot de wën wäh,*
*Ɣen them jɔ̈ï dië emennë!*
*Rieny puot kit ke ye meth,*
*Aluel Malang Deng-Awan, këdit amit daai kɔc,*
*Thiaŋ ke tuŋ në miou,*
*Kerjɔk, tuŋ atolok, tuŋ akac-haak,*
*Tuŋ aciëkkë thiɔ, ku ka ciekke meec!*

Which is literally translated as:
*Grey-white cow! The cow of my stepbrother!*
*The white perfect, the perfect to my stepbrother,*
*I can try my youth-hood right now!*
*How I shaped the perfect's color while it was still young,*
*The red cow of Malang Deng-Awan, great attracts people's eyes,*
*Stain its horns with ghee,*
*The black and white bull, horns' triumph and exclamation!*
*Its horns are as if they are near, but they are far!*

As the animals were almost to catch Nyijiny, she took a U-turn and jumped into the nearby river while carrying the *agaŋ-rial* and she was carried off by the powerful water current to a safer location next to the cattle camp. And she then trekked to the cattle camp and was warmly welcomed by her brother, relatives and friends. Her brother wholeheartedly praised her for being that determined and courageous enough to bring back the forgotten *agaŋ-rial*. She then gave her brother the *agaŋ-rial* and narrated the difficult occurrences that had befallen her on her way back to the cattle camp to him.

Upon hearing the terrifying story, his brother then informed his sister about the death of his friend's father that happened suddenly when she was still away, and he had given out their only leather sheet for placing on the deceased!

However, Deng was then triggered to retaliate on his friend's deed and decided to claim back his leather sheet that his friend's father corpse was placed on after handing over the forgotten *aɡaŋ-rial* to the owner! Consequently, this was a sort of surprise to Deng's friend who hesitated afterwards to response to his friend's demand until the elders interfered by instructing him to give back the issued leather sheet to the owner. In the end, the body to Deng's father was then exhumed and the leather sheet was taken out of the grave and given back to the owner who afterwards sliced it into pieces and threw them away!

# 92

## The Marabou Stork and The Fox

Once upon a time in the birds' kingdom, there lived a marabou stork with his wives along the Sudd swamps. One day, a friend to marabou stork, the fox visited them, and they lived for months. As required by the customs, the marabou stork and the fox suggested that they would dye their hair.

They collected the cow dung ashes (*arop*); however, the fox secretly collected the gum for destroying his friend's good-looking hair. In the process of decorating their hair, the marabou stork smartly worked on his friend's hair and the fox then took a turn to work on the marabou stork's hair. And he unexpectedly plastered glue on his friend's hair.

And in the evening, the marabou stork complained of a severe pain over his head, and he asked the fox to remove the dye! The plastered substance was then removed, and the marabou stork's hair was also lost in the process of removing the gum. The marabou's stork did not show his anger after he had realized that his hair had been intentionally removed and he inwardly thought of revenging his friend's bad intentions.

The marabou stork gave an imaginary explanation about the heaven and its glories and he invited the fox for a ride to the amazing town. The marabou stork instructed the fox to hold him firmly by his leg as he carried his friend to the said city. They took off earlier in the morning to the sky and after they had reached far, the marabou stork urged the fox to shift his hands to his other leg! While the fox was ready to grab his friend's other leg, the marabou stork cunningly dragged his leg the other direction for the fox to fall off.

Unfortunately, the fox lost his control and he falls off from the grab and he prayed: "God, let me fall into a river and let my nuts fall onto dry land." Luckily, the fox's prayers were answered, and he fall into a mud until only his head could be seen and his nuts fall in a dry location.

A cow came to drink some water and the fox asked for a pull: "Cow, you claimed to be stronger, could you manage pull me out where I have burrowed myself?" The cow came to prove her strength, but she could not manage to pull the fox out of the mud. The antelope (*Thiaŋ*) also came and tried his level best, but he did not manage to pull him out.

The elephant finally came for a drink and got the stranded fox and he instantly pulled it out and rinsed him before he placed him where his nuts were. And he found his nuts infested by the black ants. Unforgivably, he ate the pest-ridden nuts and that was when the black ants started to live in him!

# 93

The Open-Bill Stork's Problems

Long ago at the swamps, there lived an open bill stork (*Adu-nguek*). *Adu-nguek* lives on fish and frogs. One day, while he was fishing, he pounced on the electric fish (*deer*) and quickly swallowed it! Due to the great electric shock from the fish, he wailed in pain and asked: "Who has thrown a ball of fire into the fishing pond? The stuff that I had swallowed could either be a ball of fire or a melted metal!" Out of surprise, his fellow fisher bird responded: "What do you mean *Adu-nguek?* A fire could not glow beneath the water!"

He flew out of the fishing pond and sat under a tree and bewailed: "If it does not make me deaf, then it will make me mad!" The fox joined *Adu-nguek* and sympathized with him. After the fox had seen *Adu-nguek* had settled, he threw his burning question: "Have you ever caught any shark?" And *Adu-nguek* responded: "No, I have never, ever caught any shark." And the fox urged *Adu-nguek* to come with him as they go fishing for the shark.

Within the fishpond, the fox vertically aligned many tiny sticks to signal the movement of the fish (shark) and he said: "Whenever the arranged sticks get swayed, that signals the passage of the greatest fish.

However, when the fish passes, a few of the aligned sticks are pushed down and that is the very target which you can aim at and spear immediately."

And the fox continued to coach *Adu-nguek*: "When it comes to the shark's passageway, the nearby grasses together with the aligned sticks are all pushed down. And you should not directly spear it instantly when the aligned sticks are pushed down; but spear it when the shark's movement is almost to its last."

The advice was well received by the *Adu-nguek* and the fox left him ready with his beak positioned at the aligned tiny sticks as he waited for the coming of a shark. The fox then wrapped a huge stone with a net and dived carrying it towards the location where he left *Adu-nguek* standing. After a while, the fox reached the site where the sticks were aligned, and he successfully passed through them and *Adu-nguek* did not hit onto him and the movement continued until the wrapped stone finally reached when the movement was almost to its last and *Adu-nguek* hastily struck the great stone and its beak got curved.

# 94

*Casted Spell*

Once upon a time, there lived many varieties of birds along the Nile Basin. The birds lived in groups, fished together and spent most of their jolly times in clusters as they enjoyed eating many types of fish.

One day, the birds arranged their fishing excursion along the shallow waters of the River Nile. As they were fishing, ibis *(Arum-joh)* caught a fish and exclaimed: "Majok-Arum!" Meaning, 'his black and white bull' and he caught many fish within those few minutes whereas the other birds did not kill any! Nevertheless, marabou stork *(dheel)* felt jealous as to why he was not killing any fish!

However, he thought of grabbing the *Arum-joh's* fish next time when he kills an extra fish! After a while, *Arum-joh* caught his fish and *Dheel* immediately rushed to snatch it from him but *Arum-joh* dodged him. Therefore, *dheel* badly beat *Arum-joh* on his back until the innocent bird became unconscious and *Dheel* seized the fish and ate it impatiently.

And Adada Ibis *(Awuwau)* screamed: *"Ka ber ya Raan?"* Which is literally translated: 'Would it come back to life again?' The other birds got concern and they ferried the poor bird to the riverbank leaving

*Dheel* only stroking in the waters. *Arum-Joh* then recovered from the shockwave but had trouble whenever he breathes. That is why *Arum-joh* experiences a whizzing sound whenever he breathes!

And the big-black-bird-polyvore *(Agaal)* cast his spell: *"Toŋë, na cie lɔ rɔm miak, ke xen cie jam nyok!"* Which is literally translated as: 'If this war does not break out tomorrow, I will never ever speak a word for the rest of my life!' Anyway, the war did not break out the following morning and Agaal, became dumb.

# 95

## *The Elephant's Garden and The Fox*

M any years ago, the elephant had a big garden next to the river. One day, the fox thought of going hunting and he accidentally found the elephant expanding his garden. And the fox visibly watched the elephant as he ploughed his farm at his hide out. The fox then bathed in mud and went home and deceived his wife that he had relentlessly been working on their farm the whole day. And his wife applauded him for his hard work before he was showered.

As the fox and his wife were conversing, the breadwinner assured his wife that he would return to their farm the following day. And as planned, his wife woke up earlier that morning and prepared a meal for her husband who would then go to their farm. The fox ate his food and left for a hunt pretending to be going out for farming!

The elephant went to his farm earlier as usual and enthusiastically ploughed a huge piece of land. He worked for a whole day until he completed ploughing his garden. And in the evening, the fox passed by the elephant's garden and bathed in mud as usual to indicate that he had tirelessly been working on his garden before returning home. He was then welcomed by his wife who afterwards fetched his water for bathing. And the fox gladly declared that he had completed ploughing their great farm.

After three months, the fox paid a visit to the elephant's farm and found out that the planted cereals were ready to be harvested. He then detached some maize cobs and carried them to his home. His wife felt happy to have received the freshest maize cobs. The following day, the fox woke up before the cock crowed and went to the elephant's garden to bring home some more farm products. And he made it to steal the farm produce once again.

Afterwards, the elephant found out that his crops were not in order; some pumpkins and maize cobs were missing! Consequently, the elephant decided to produce a scarecrow (made of sticky gum) to keep the intruders away or catch the perpetrators. Earlier the next day, the fox came again to steal more farm produce and found the scarecrow. He had never ever seen a scarecrow, and as a result, he went next to it and asked: "What are you doing in my garden?" But the scarecrow did not respond.

Hence, the fox got annoyed to the extent that he could pick up a stick and hit the scarecrow, but the stick got stuck in the sticky gum. And he slapped the scarecrow and his hand got stuck too in the gum, and he slapped it again using his left hand and it was also caught by the gum. He then kicked it with his right leg and the gum did not also release it. However, he tried with his left leg winning and it was in the end held firmly by the gum. And the fox remained glued onto the scarecrow until the following morning when the elephant came and found him captured. He then collected some caning sticks and beat the sly animal until it became unconscious before he could pardon him.

# 96

### The Trick Within A Trick

In the ancient days, a renowned fox who had experience in traditional medical processes was invited by the lion's family to do some operations on their grandmother. The lions had the trick of capturing the fox alive as he had tricked every animal in the woods.

The lions collected mud and covered their grandmother's knee with it to deceive the sly animal! The mud was suitably molded across her knees in such a way that it could accommodate some sour milk *(miɔh)* which looks like pus! After they had completed putting some final touches around her knee, they sent one of their articulate sons to inform the fox that the fox was needed by his father to come and carry out an operation on their grandmother's swollen knee.

The child went and delivered the expected message to the fox as demanded and the fox replied: "This information is noted and received with thanks; I will come to your home soon." The child then returned to their home and relayed the message that the fox had accepted to come and carry out the operation on their grandmother's knees.

The fox afterwards started his journey to the lions' home and on his way, he knotted many tall grasses at spaced intervals along the path to block the lions whenever they chase him. Besides the secured knots, the fox had already dug his tunnel as his alternative hide out.

After some minutes' walk, the fox reached the lions' homestead and found many lions standing around their grandmother who was seated on a stool. The fox then stood far away and waved at them from a relatively far distance. And after the lions had seen that the fox was not ready to join them, one of the sons to the grandmother explained once again the reason as to why they called him: "My grandmother's knee is swollen and needs to be operated, can you please come closer and work on it?"

The fox afterwards went closer to the said patient and urged everyone to extend back a bit so that he should be able to dodge the dripping pus during the operation processes. And the lions extended themselves back as demanded by the fox.

Just after some few seconds, the fox removed his scalpel (*pal*) and punctured the molded segment at their grandmother's knee and then dropped the *pal* before he swiftly ran away. No sooner did the lions saw the fox piercing the formed area, than they quickly ran towards him to seize him. The other lions tried their best to grab him, but they were obstructed by the intertwined knots on the way. Eventually, the fox overran the lions and sped away and entered his tunnel whose exit was situated deep in the jungle.

Over there in the forest, the fox found a gigantic honey base in a groove and he instantly used a trick of harvesting it. The fox strategically dipped his tail into one of the nearby waters ponds and skillfully approached the bees' furrow and placed the dripping tail into the groove and the soaked tail proximately attracted several bees. And after he had seen that many bees had landed on his tail, he gently carried the bees far away and swayed them off from his tail; and he dispersed the quaffing insects before he could return to the very site! The fox repeatedly did these five times until he could complete ferrying away the swamps of bees before he happily picked and carried home the unprotected honey.

# 97

### The Guests Welcoming Mother

O nce upon a time in one of the less populated village, there lived an old lady named Man-Deng Akuem. Man-Deng Akuem was left by her husband and children who then went to the cattle camp but left her alone at home.

Man Deng-Akuem was fond of welcoming visitors who happened to be passing by her home at late hours. However, the ogre secretly monitored the old woman's generosity and thought of exploiting the opportunity. The old lady had been welcoming visitors for many decades before she changed her mind not to welcome the strangers into her house.

One evening, an ogre pretended to be on his journey and passed next to Man-Deng Akuem's homestead and he was immediately welcomed by the kind-hearted woman into her hut, and they chatted for a while with the ogre before they could sleep. In the process of their conversation, the stranger changed himself into an ogre and asked the old lady: "If I eat you right now, who will help you out?" And Man-Deng Akuem replied: "Surely, you will eat me after I have put on my jewelry that I left outside before." And the ogre pardoned the destitute lady to go out and collect her jewelry. Afterwards, Man-Deng Akuem rushed out and hid herself in the cover crop; pumpkins and she was not found by the ogre who then left and went on his way before the daybreak.

The following morning, the ogre returned in form of a human being and asked Man-Deng Akuem: "Where did you sleep yester-night?" And she replied: "I slept in the cover crop, pumpkins." And the ogre applauded: "It is a good place for you to sleep in; continue sleeping over there!" And the old lady responded: "Yes, I will keep on sleeping over there."

That night, the old lady changed her sleeping position and hid herself in the beans growth and she was not found by the ogre that night when he keenly searched for her in the cover crop of pumpkins. The next morning, the ogre came again in form of a human being and asked Man-Deng Akuem: "Where did you sleep yesternight?" And Man-Deng Akuem replied: "I slept in the beans growth." And the ogre commended: "It is a good place to sleep in, continue sleeping over there!" And the old lady responded: "Yes, I will keep on sleeping over there."

The next night, Man-Deng Akuem changed her sleeping position and she covered herself with grasses and laid herself across the road that comes to her home. And the ogre came following the very path and stumbled onto her and she yelled: "What a big tree across the path!" And the poor woman remained calm!

The ogre proceeded to Man-Deng Akuem's home and searched for her everywhere in her compound, but he did not find her. The subsequent morning, the ogre returned in form of a human being and asked Man-Deng Akuem: "Where did you sleep yester-night?" And she replied: "I covered myself with grasses and laid myself across the road that comes to my house and you even stumbled onto me when you were coming." And the ogre applauded: "It is a good place to sleep in, continue sleeping over there!" And the old lady responded: "Yes, I will keep on sleeping over there."

The following night, the old lady hid herself inside a South Sudanese mortar and the ogre came and searched for her everywhere in the compound and along the paths, but she was nowhere to be found! The ogre then sat on a mortar and he rested. While he was resting, Man-Deng Akuem pinched one the ogre's buttocks and he complained: "Ouch! What a black ant that has pinched my buttock so severely!"

The following morning, the ogre came again in form of a human being and asked Man-Deng Akuem: "Where did you sleep last night?" And she replied: "I hid myself inside a South Sudanese mortar and I pinched you on your buttock as you were resting on it." And the ogre commended: "It is a good place to sleep in, continue sleeping over there!" And the old lady responded: "Yes, I will keep on sleeping over there."

Consequently, the ogre made it to Man-Deng Akuem's home in the evening and asked her: "Since I have found you before you could hide yourself this evening, what will make you escape now?" And Man-Deng responded: "Yes, you will eat me right now but look over there at my sons who are just returning home from the cattle camp!" The ogre looked at the pointed direction and saw many black moving pictures of big-black-birds-polyvores (agäl) which really appeared like people! The ogre trembled and asked the old lady: "Where will I seek a refuge from the approaching youth?" And the old wise lady suggested: "Just rush to the nearby open field and you will find a small hole in the middle of the pitch; and you can hide yourself inside it!" The ogre hurriedly ran to the said field and unwittingly dashed into the well and that was when the old lady was set free!

# 98

## The Liver-Craving Wife

Once upon a time, there lived a man and his newly married wife, and the spouses loved each other so much. After five years of their marriage, they were blessed with a baby girl and a baby boy. Thereafter, his wife had a month pregnancy, but she refused to eat other foods other than liver! However, she did not experience such a craving desire of eating liver in her other preceding pregnancies.

Her husband slaughtered a goat, and its liver was cooked for her. However, she only ate a half of her food before she discontinued eating the food! Her family members daily cooked a domestic animal's liver for her for almost two months when she developed a low appetite of eating liver from all domesticated animals.

The next day, she ordered her husband to hunt wild animals for their liver as her appetite for eating liver increased. The husband wholeheartedly agreed and hunted wild animals and brought back a variety of livers to appease his wife, but all was in vain. Nevertheless, she did refuse eating the liver that she had eaten once eaten! In so doing, her husband continued hunting for three months before he completed killing all the animals except the lion which he feared to attack.

A few days later, the husband returned from his hunt with a liver of an antelope whose liver was once eaten by his wife, but the woman refused to eat it but instructed her husband to bring for her a lion's liver! The husband was puzzled and hastily breathed both cold and warm air!

The husband desperately accepted her request and left for the jungle to hunt the dreadful lion. It then took him six hours before he finally found a lion. He swiftly rushed for it and tactfully speared the lion in the chest. The lion maneuvered to clench the hunter and the hunter encountered the beast by spearing the lion sideways but the lion resisted the piercing and furiously tore the hunter into fragments!

# 99

## The Greedy Man's Misfortune

Long ago, there lived a man named Deng and his wives, Man-Atong and Man-Ayak in their rural village of Pur-rap. And his wives lived close by at their separate homes. Man-Atong and Man-Ayak were all industrious except their husband, Deng. They were very caring and cooperative and so did their children.

The two wives cooked in turns in which each of them did cook twice a day as an irrevocable order from their gluttonous husband who did eat at the interval of four hours a day. Both wives were regularly active and punctual. From their timetable, Man-Atong cooked food was served at 7:00 AM and 3:00 PM while Man-Ayak's food was served at 11:00 AM and 7:00 PM.

Deng and his family members cordially put up among themselves and their neighbors. Two years later, they had a good harvest for both simsim and ground nuts on their separate farms. That evening after they had collected their farm produce, Deng instructed his wives to prepare for him both simsim and ground nuts four times a day and the women did as they were told.

In the evening before he ate his fourth meal, Deng felt very thirsty, and he drunk a lot of water until he emptied all the water gourds at his home but that did not quench his thirst! Subsequently, he rushed to the nearby stream to engulf plenty of water as much as he wanted to quench his thirst. He drank for some minutes before his stomach dilated and got burst! One of the witnesses went and conveyed the sad news to the bereaved wife and she burst into her song:

*Man-Atong, baar Man-Ayak pande!*
*Ye ŋo kua tieŋ-moidie?*
*Deng monyda acie thou!*
*Thïethiei! Thïethiei!*
*Rïnyden acïe beer ŋoot!*
*Acïn rïnyden ber tou!*

Which is literally translated as:
*Mother to Atong, come along with the mother to Ayak from her home,*
*What is the matter my co-wife?*
*Deng, our husband has died!*
*Blessings! Blessings!*
*His age mates had all perished!*
*No one among his age mates is still alive!*

The neighbors were all annoyed as to why the wives to the deceased sang and danced immediately when they heard the sad news of their own husband's departure! However, the wives stopped singing their delightful songs after they detected their neighbors' annoyance written on their faces!

Afterwards, people rushed to the site, recovered Deng's body and buried him next to his house and everyone then left with a sooty heart. That night, Deng wives had an unrestful night. Their husband came to them in a dream and repeatedly ask them: "Why were you that excited after the fate stroke me?" And the wives yelled throughout the whole night until the following morning!

Earlier the next day, the wives to the deceased invited their relatives and neighbors to their house and they had slaughtered a bull. The invited relatives and guests then prayed for forgiveness for the two widows before they finally feasted. After the departure of the invited relatives and guests, their husband didn't haunt the two wives again in the form of dreams that night.

# 100

## *The Stepmother*

In the oldest day, there lived a man who had two wives. One day, fate took one of his wives and left a boy and a girl behind with their stepmother. The girl, Achol was the eldest while the boy, Deng was the youngest. They lived a miserable life as they were treated badly by their stepmother.

Their stepmother overworked Achol who was in good relationship with her age mates. The stepmother disrespected her stepchildren and spent less time with them to befriend them. This made the children lose their hope but live a lonely life!

One day, Achol thought of abandoning her stepmother and venturing into an unknown destiny. She decided to bid all her age mates her final goodbye before she could embark on her solitary journey. She then informed her age mates that she would disown her family and start her own life. Achol did treat her friends with respect and courtesy therefore, all her age mates pledged to go with her wherever she was going and live together.

Few days later in the morning, Achol and her friends left for the jungle and embarked on a desperate expedition. They walked for a whole day till sun set and could not make it to maneuver through a thick and a dark forest that night and they opted to find a place where they could spend a night.

They eventually found a place and sat there and Achol decided to evoke her ancestral spirit to descend for a divine help. Achol went on and said: "If you are a land of my ancestors, I instruct you to provide us with cattle's barn full of cattle and huts!" No sooner did the Achol ended the chant, than the cattle's barn full of cattle and three huts came forth and all the girls were happy for the divine gift! Achol and her friends then milked their cows and consumed the milk.

The girls slept afterwards, and the pride of lions came and asked:

*Achol, ca dïn?*
*Ka cïe nyïnydu yëndï?*
*Ku mɛn can bɛ̈n, bï ŋo yëndï?*
*Ca nin? yɛn kën nin.*
*yɛn tɔ̈u në tiɔp de kuärkuɔ nhom.*

Which is translated as:
*Achol, are you mad?*
*Or what had happened to your senses?*
*As I have come, what do you think will happen?*
*Have you slept? No, I have not slept yet.*
*I am on my ancestral land.*

The lions kept on disturbing Achol the whole night until daybreak when they finally left. This repeatedly happened for two consecutive nights. And on the third night, Achol woke her colleagues up so that they may hear it by themselves what the lions were saying! And the girls were much terrified and could not sleep again until morning when they ran back to their respective homes leaving Achol alone in the jungle.

One of the girls went home and informed Deng, Achol's brother that the lions disturbed them whole night and all the girls had run away leaving Achol alone in the forest. Deng equipped himself with his fighting tools and ran toward the said location. He followed the path until he coincidentally located where his sister was residing! He then urged his sister to leave with him to go back home and her sister questioned: "If I return home, will our stepmother not mistreat us again?" And Achol's brother answered: "We will go and settle separately at our own home."

Within those few minutes of their talks, Achol pleaded face up and intoned: "If you are the land of our ancestors, I hereby beseech that my brother, all my cattle, cattle barn, huts and I will be moved instantly to our village!" Surprisingly, all her wishes came to pass, and the villagers welcomed them back with their belongings!

# 101

## The Honest Bride

Once upon a time, there lived an industrious girl named Nyantiop in a rural village of Angongdu. Nyantiop was an honest girl who frankly revealed to men that she did eat a lot. However, the men quitted engaging her after they learned about her super appetite!

One day, a man named Maker approached her and Nyantiop disclosed as usual that she had a scaring appetite. After hearing that, Maker insisted on marrying her despite her eating habit. Nyantiop finally endorsed Maker's proposal and they were in their courtship for nine months before their traditional marriage was arranged by their parents.

After the completion of their customary marriage processes, the bride was accompanied to her new home by her relatives and friends. Earlier the following morning, a bull was slaughtered for the guests as specified by their culture. When the visitors' cooked meal was ready, they were served with hot stew. However, the bride hungrily consumed a large share of the meal leaving her colleagues with empty stomach and the same incident repeated itself in the evening!

The following morning, the visitors reported that their time of returning to their respective homes had come and they were pardoned

to leave by Nyantiop's brothers-in-law leaving Nyantiop alone in
her home. However, Nyantiop's sisters-in-law were not aware of her
great appetite and they cooked a little food thinking that it would be
enough for her! Nyantiop hastily ate it in agony and sneaked out of
her new home and returned to her parents' home that evening after
she was given little food to eat!

She reached her mother's home and frankly narrated to her mother all the encounters she had faced while in her new home. And her
mother immediately cooked for her enough food and she excitedly
ate it until she was satisfied. Her husband, Maker realized that his wife
was nowhere to be seen at home. He was concerned about his wife
disappearance and he decided to look for his wife's whereabouts at
her relatives' homes and he firstly came to Nyantiop's maternal aunt
and asked:

*Kudualdun pan de Malen!*
*Kudualdu eya. Ye yïn ŋa?*
*Ee yen Maker. Maker, ye kän-ŋo cïn ya cath waköw?*
*Ee Nyantiop yen ka cie jal baai! Nyantiop akën bën enoŋ wuok?*
*Liëpke yen hot! Te cen bën, ee dï chuku lëk yïn!*
*Liëpkë yen höt!*
*Ye këda ya chuër, kua ye ruɔ̈m?*

Which is literally translated as:
*Greetings to you, maternal aunt!*
*Greetings to you too? Who are you?*
*I am Maker. Maker, why are you traveling overnight?*
*Is Nyantiop who has just left her home. Nyantiop has not come to us.*
*Open for me the door please! If she had come, we would have told you!*
*Open for me the door please! Is ours a thievery plan or a robbery?*

Nevertheless, Maker searched for his lost wife at many of her close
relatives' homes, but he did not find her. Maker asked for his lost wife
at her uncle's, stepmother's and her elder brother's residences but she

was not found only that the above statements were replies heard from all the in-laws. As a result, he finally returned to his mother-in-law's home and boldly asked for his wife again: "Nyantiop, I know you are currently staying with your mother, can you please come out?"

No sooner did Maker seriously demanded his wife to come out of the hut, than Nyantiop's mother instructed her daughter to get out of their hut while carrying her big eating calabash. Amazingly, Maker was really impressed to see his wife once more in a person. The two conversed for a while before they returned to their home. At home, Maker ordered his sisters to milk all the cows and cook enough food for his wife before he gathered his relatives and disclosed his wife's eating habit! All his family members collectively participated by contributing enough cows, grains, ghee, beans and other food stuffs for Maker's family.

Some days later, one of Maker's eldest uncles suggested that Nyantiop should start cooking her own family food and oversee the contributed households' resources and that was the best decision in handling Nyantiop's excessive eating habit. She felt contented and joined her husband in ploughing their gardens that were extended by many feddans. Four months later, they harvested a lot of farm produce from their gardens and they greatly enjoyed the fruits of their labor.

# 102

## The Choice is in Your Hands

Long ago, there lived a young man who wanted to challenge an old wise man. He caught a bird, held it behind his back, approached the old man and asked him: "Oh uncle, is the bird that I am holding in my hands behind me dead or alive?"

He thought to himself as it would be a good opportunity to test the wise man's cleverness. If the old man says the bird is alive, he will simply squeeze its neck! And if he says the bird is dead, the boy will simply let it fly away!

The wise old man instantly uncovered the trick and tasked the young boy: "My dear son, the answer to your question is in your own hands!" And the boy held his head down in recognition.

And the old man continued to speak: "Remember my boy, harmony and conflict, penalty and mercy, moral and immoral are always in your hands! It is not your cleverness but the route of your intellect that governs the track of your life! Always remember, that all the people have the control to do good and evil! There is always a choice, and the choice is in your own hands!

CPSIA information can be obtained
at www.ICGtesting.com
Printed in the USA
LVHW031809090721
692281LV00003B/309